Matrix: The Impossible Decision

José Antonio González Villalón
Synergy AI Tech Solutions, LLC

I0662113

Legal Notice / Disclaimer

This work is a work of fiction.

While it draws inspiration from organizational dynamics, corporate decision-making, and transformation processes commonly found in large and complex enterprises, it does not describe real events, nor does it intend to represent any specific individuals, companies, governments, or institutions.

All characters, names, titles, organizational structures, events, and situations depicted in this book are fictional creations intended solely for literary and reflective purposes. Any total or partial resemblance to real persons, living or deceased, or to existing, past, or future organizations is purely coincidental.

References to systems, processes, colors, governance structures, regions, industries, or operating models do not correspond to, nor allude to, real products, vendors, or implementations. They are used exclusively as narrative devices to explore universal themes related to leadership, decision-making, power, organizational change, and transparency.

This book does not constitute professional advice of any kind, including technical, financial, legal, accounting, or management advice. The ideas presented should not be interpreted as specific recommendations for system implementation, technology selection, or the execution of transformation initiatives within real organizations.

The author does not assert or imply the existence of misconduct, irregularities, unlawful behavior, or improper intent on the part of any real individuals or organizations. The conflicts, tensions, and dilemmas portrayed are elements of a fictional narrative intended to illustrate human and structural challenges that may arise in complex contexts.

By reading this work, the reader acknowledges and accepts that its purpose is literary and reflective in nature, not documentary, investigative, or testimonial.

The term "Matrix" is used in its conceptual and metaphorical sense, as a representation of a framework of thought or a system of beliefs, and bears no relation to existing cinematic or literary works.

The name "Project Matrix" is used solely as a narrative and metaphorical device. Projects with similar names exist across multiple organizations and are unrelated to one another.

Author's Note for Executive Readers

This book should not be read as a critique of past, present, or future decisions, but as an invitation to reflect on the non-technical factors that influence high-impact strategic decisions. Technology serves here as a symbol; the true tensions explored are human, cultural, and ethical.

INDICE

Author's Preface

This book did not begin as a novel.

It began as an uncomfortable question.

Over the years, I have participated—directly or indirectly—in decisions that are often presented as technical, yet in reality define the direction, culture, and transparency of entire organizations. Decisions that are frequently summarized in a single, deceptively simple word: system.

With time, I came to understand that systems are rarely the true problem.

They are the mirror.

The stories told here do not describe real events or specific organizations. They do not seek to assign blame, nor to offer universal solutions. They are works of fiction inspired by patterns that recur within large, complex, and global enterprises— environments where power, institutional memory, and resistance coexist in subtle and often unspoken ways.

These patterns do not originate from a single experience or a particular case. They emerge from personal observations, conversations with colleagues, shared accounts from professionals in the field of information technology, and insights accumulated over years across different organizational contexts. They are not rooted in any specific company or current situation, but in recurring dynamics that transcend names, geographies, and moments in time.

Any resemblance to real individuals, organizations, or processes is the result of a shared reality, not an intention to portray.

This book does not aim to explain how to implement an ERP, nor to defend one technology over another. It does not seek to discredit past decisions. On the contrary, it is grounded in deep respect for those who sustained organizations for years through imperfect solutions, creative adaptations, and tacit agreements that made growth possible.

The central question is not which system to choose.

The question is what happens when an organization decides to see itself without filters.

Throughout these pages, dilemmas rarely discussed openly are explored: the fear of transparency, the invisible cost of not deciding, the fragility of poorly executed transformations, and the human burden carried by those who attempt to bring order to what functioned for years without explicit structure.

If this book feels uncomfortable, it has fulfilled its purpose.

Not because it reveals hidden truths, but because it invites the reader to recognize that many "impossible" decisions are not impossible due to a lack of information, but because of an excess of implications.

This is not a story about technology.

It is a story about leadership in the face of truth.

And about the courage—or the absence of it—required to stand by decisions once they cease to be popular.

Prologue — The Assassination of the Emperor

No one in the Empire remembered a morning so silent.

It was not an official announcement that broke the calm. There was no alarm, no urgent communication. It was something more subtle: a series of meetings canceled without explanation, an empty calendar where decisions normally lived, and a rumor that spread without the need for words.

The Emperor had fallen.

There was no blood.

No public scandal.

No visible betrayal.

And yet, everyone knew.

For years, the Empire had lived under the illusion of stability. The numbers appeared to support the narrative, the provinces grew in their own ways, and Olympus—that council of ancient founders and newly risen gods—watched from above, confident that the system would continue to function as it always had.

Until it didn't.

The poor results of the last cycle were not an accident. Nor were those of the cycle before it. Or the one before that. They were the inevitable consequence of a fragmented Empire, governed by different rules in each territory, sustained by systems that no longer spoke to one another, and by truths that shifted depending on who told them.

For a long time, that fragmentation had been defended as a virtue. Autonomy, they called it. Flexibility. Local adaptability. Each province was expected to find its own path, its own way of growing, its own interpretation of the business. The Capital, noble in its intent, had allowed this doctrine to harden into dogma.

The Emperor inherited an Empire already divided.

He did not build it that way, but he ruled within those constraints. In his early years, he believed that gradual adjustments would suffice— tactical improvements, small initiatives that addressed visible problems without questioning the entire architecture. Preserving peace was easier than rewriting the rules.

But peace came at a cost.

The debt was not only technological. It was cultural. Operational. Political. Each isolated system, each reinterpreted report, each local exception accepted without challenge added another layer of invisible complexity. No one could see the Empire as a whole without distortion. No one could say, with absolute certainty, where value was created and where it was lost.

When results began to deteriorate consistently, rhetoric was no longer enough.

That was when the Emperor accepted what he had long avoided: consulting the Oracle.

It was not an impulsive decision. Nor an act of faith. It was a quiet acknowledgment that the Empire had passed the point where intuition alone was sufficient. The Oracle did not promise magical solutions. It promised something far more dangerous: clarity.

The Oracle did not speak in absolutes.

It spoke in scenarios.

It revealed possible paths, real costs, and unavoidable consequences. Above all, it revealed something that deeply unsettled Olympus: a shared truth—a single reading of the Empire, without regional exceptions or convenient interpretations.

The prophecy was clear.

The Empire had to choose.

Not between systems.

Not between vendors.

But between two ways of existing.

Fragmented continuity... or unified transformation.

For some of the gods of Olympus, the prophecy was received with genuine interest. For others, with caution. And for a few, with a discomfort they dared not express aloud. A unified Empire would require the surrender of silent privileges: control over local narratives, the ability to explain results according to context, the protection that ambiguity provides.

The decision was not announced immediately. Like all uncomfortable truths, it was allowed to rest, to be analyzed, to be questioned. Endless meetings were convened. Second opinions were requested. Alternatives were compared—options that appeared different, yet all avoided the same central issue: the need for a single version of the truth.

In the Eastern provinces, the reaction was different.

There, the prophecy was not seen as an opportunity, but as a threat. The system that had accompanied them for years provided more than operations; it provided identity. It had grown with them, adapted to their rules, and allowed a degree of freedom that an imperial system would never grant.

A unified Empire meant something more dangerous than change.

It meant transparency.

And transparency, like any intense light, does not distinguish between honest mistakes and carefully constructed narratives.

From across the sea, messages began to arrive—laden with concern. Not explicit. Not confrontational. But persistent. There, they said, reality was different. Time zones, regulations, culture, markets. There, a vision born in the Capital could not be imposed. There, the prophecy did not apply.

Meanwhile, in the Capital, the Emperor was beginning to stand alone.

Not for lack of loyalty, but for an excess of caution. Some gods of Olympus agreed with the need for change, yet feared the political cost. Others were not ready to relinquish the comfort of an Empire that, while imperfect, still functioned well enough to avoid open rupture.

Support for the Emperor did not vanish overnight.

It eroded.

Like air escaping a sealed room—slowly, silently—until breathing became impossible.

Olympus convened one final time without him.

Not to judge.

Not to confront.

But to replace him.

The assassination was clean. Political. Irrevocable.

There was no dramatic announcement, no solemn speech. Only an orderly transition, wrapped in words such as renewal, a new chapter, and vision for the future. The Emperor left the throne without resistance, fully aware that his fate had been sealed the moment he allowed the Oracle to speak.

When the news was confirmed, the Empire was suspended in a strange moment: the most important decision in its history had already been made... but the leader meant to carry it out was no longer there.

In the corridors of the Capital, no one knew what would come next. In the provinces, some breathed in relief, others remained alert. The Oracle still stood, untouched, waiting for someone with the courage to fulfill the prophecy.

The Empire had lost its Emperor.

But the decision remained alive.

And now, for the first time in decades, the Empire had to ask itself whether it possessed the courage to face a shared truth...

—or whether it would choose to continue living inside its own Matrix.

Chapter 1 — When the Family Stopped Governing

The Empire was not always an Empire.

For a long time, it was simply a family.

A family that had learned to grow through intuition, constant work, and fast decisions. The first plants emerged almost out of necessity: to produce more, deliver better, and meet the demands of clients who were growing at the same pace. There were no master plans or long-term architectures. There was trust. There was proximity. There was direct control.

The founders knew every corner of the business. They knew who made decisions, who solved problems, and who was accountable. Important conversations did not require minutes or committees. A table, a cup of coffee, and the natural authority of those who had built the Empire from nothing were enough.

That model worked... until it didn't.

Growth outpaced the ability to govern it. New plants, new countries, new cultures. What had once been closeness began to turn into distance. Decisions could no longer be made in a single language or within a single time zone. The family understood, with clarity, that the Empire had outgrown the stage at which it could be run as a family business.

That was when they stepped aside.

They did not abandon the Empire. They did not sell their legacy. They simply stopped governing directly. They withdrew to Olympus, convinced that their role was now to safeguard the vision, not to execute the day-to-day.

From Olympus, the family continued to observe. To influence. But no longer to intervene in every decision. That space was filled by professional executives—leaders trained to manage complexity, not to found empires.

The change was necessary.

But it was also the beginning of something no one fully anticipated.

With the family's withdrawal from direct governance, a new doctrine was born: the doctrine of independence.

Each plant, each region, each new acquisition was to be free to develop its maximum potential. The Capital was not to become a bottleneck. The Empire was not to suffocate local innovation with rigid rules. The philosophy sounded sensible, even modern. It was the language of books, conferences, and global management best practices.

Autonomy.

Empowerment.

Decisions close to the business.

And for a time, it worked.

The provinces grew rapidly. Europe expanded through strategic acquisitions. Asia opened paths in complex markets. North America consolidated operations with pragmatism. Each territory developed its own way of operating, of measuring success, and of explaining results.

The Capital watched with pride.

What no one noticed—or chose not to notice—was that this autonomy was not accompanied by a shared framework. There was no clear imperial architecture. No common long-term vision of what the Empire was meant to look like in ten or twenty years. Each province interpreted independence as sovereignty.

And sovereignty, once granted, is difficult to reclaim.

Technology was one of the first territories where fragmentation became visible.

In the Capital, the central system had evolved alongside the Empire. It was not perfect, but it was robust. It had survived crises, mergers, regulatory changes, and operational transformations. More importantly, the knowledge lived within the Empire. The team that sustained it did not depend on third parties to understand it. They knew where to intervene—and, above all, where not to.

That knowledge was not fully documented. It could not be. It was living knowledge, accumulated through years of real operations, corrected mistakes, and long nights solving problems no one else saw.

It was the Empire's Library.

In the provinces, the story was different.

Each acquisition arrived with its own system, its own vendor, and its own logic. In Europe, one of those systems became a symbol of identity. It did more than run operations; it represented continuity, stability, and a way of working that had proven itself over time.

For them, changing that system was not evolution.

It was a threat.

The Capital respected that position. After all, the doctrine of independence demanded it. If the provinces delivered results, why intervene?

That reasoning repeated itself until it became the norm.

Over time, the Empire began to resemble less an integrated structure and more a constellation of kingdoms connected only by name and a handful of corporate rituals.

Reports traveled to the Capital, but each spoke a different language. Numbers were consolidated, but definitions varied. Results were explained through local narratives that were not always comparable.

When things went well, autonomy received the credit.

When things went poorly, it was because "they" did not understand the local reality.

The Capital, faithful to its conciliatory spirit, accepted both explanations.

It was not weakness.

It was good faith.

But good faith, without structure, becomes fragility.

Over the years, several Emperors passed through the throne. Each inherited the same fragmented Empire. Each attempted to govern it in his own way. Some reinforced autonomy. Others tried to centralize without confrontation. None resolved the underlying tension.

Until results stopped supporting the narrative.

The accumulation of small deviations—misaligned local decisions, incompatible systems, and contradictory stories—began to manifest in something impossible to ignore: the Empire's overall performance.

Explaining was no longer enough.

Justifying was no longer enough.

4

Trusting was no longer enough.

The Empire needed to see itself without filters.

That was the moment when the story changed direction.

Not because someone wanted to impose control.

But because, for the first time, the Empire realized it had lost the ability to understand itself as a whole.

And when an Empire can no longer understand itself, it can no longer govern itself.

Chapter 2 — Olympus

Olympus was not made of marble, nor did it rise above visible mountains.

It was a discreet, well-lit room, deliberately designed to appear neutral. Nothing in it announced power—and yet, everything in it concentrated it.

This was where those who no longer governed the day-to-day gathered, but who still shaped the destiny of the Empire.

The original founders occupied seats no one questioned. Not because of formal hierarchy, but because of history. Their authority was not written into any charter, yet it was felt in the way others waited for them to speak first, or in how a single sentence from them could tilt an entire conversation.

Over the years, Olympus had changed its face. New gods had joined the original ones: external advisors, representatives from acquired territories, figures who had not been present at the beginning but who now formed part of the Empire's political balance.

Not all of them shared the same vision.

They did not even share the same definition of success.

For some, the Empire should be a collection of profitable businesses, each optimized for its own context. For others, it should behave as a single entity—coherent, comparable, predictable. The tension between those two views was not new, but until then it had been manageable.

Olympus did not debate operations.

It debated narratives.

Meetings always began the same way: reports, results, explanations. Each territory presented its version of the state of the Empire, carefully contextualized. Words such as exceptional, temporary, and contextual appeared frequently—not as excuses, but as tools to shape perception.

For years, that system had worked. No one lied outright. Everyone simply spoke from their own reality.

The problem was that there was no longer a single reality.

The original founders observed closely. Some with genuine concern. Others with a mix of nostalgia and resignation. They had built the Empire on direct control and clear accountability. Seeing it now fragmented, explained through disconnected pieces, produced a discomfort that was difficult to put into words.

Yet they did not want to impose.

They had learned—sometimes through painful experience—that governing from the past rarely produces a future.

The addition of new gods to Olympus altered the balance.

One of them came from the Eastern Provinces. He was not a stranger to the Empire; for years, he had owned part of what had now become the whole. His presence represented continuity for those regions—a guarantee that their identity would not be absorbed by the Capital.

To him, the Empire was not a centralized construction, but a federation of distinct realities. He had grown under a local system he knew intimately, one that had supported his businesses for decades. That system was not merely a tool; it was part of his history.

Changing it was not an improvement.

It was a rupture.

From his perspective, the Capital never fully grasped the complexity of the East—its markets, regulations, ways of working. Any attempt at unification felt like a dangerous simplification, designed for the convenience of a few.

That position found resonance among other members of Olympus—not so much from technical conviction as from political caution. No one wanted to be seen as the god who forced a transformation that might endanger territories that, at least on the surface, were still functioning.

The Emperor attended those meetings with an invisible weight on his shoulders.

He knew Olympus was not a place for direct confrontation. Decisions there were not imposed; they were built through silent consensus. A gesture of disapproval, an apparently innocent question, a prolonged pause could carry more weight than any passionate speech.

For a time, he tried to preserve balance.

He listened.

He conceded.

He postponed.

But each meeting left behind a clearer sensation: Olympus was no longer aligned. There was no shared vision of the Empire's future—only temporary agreements designed to avoid conflict.

It was within that context that the Oracle began to take shape.

Not as an imposition by the Emperor, but as an elegant exit. A way to move the discussion from political ground to technical ground. A way to ask—without accusation—whether the Empire was truly prepared for the next cycle of its history.

Olympus accepted.

Not with enthusiasm, but with relief.

It was easier to request an analysis than to take a position.

Over time, however, the Oracle began to unsettle.

Not because it openly contradicted anyone, but because it eliminated gray areas. Where there had once been interpretations, there were now scenarios. Where there had once been speeches, there were now comparable numbers. The language became more precise—and precision, in Olympus, was dangerous.

Some gods began to ask different questions. Not about costs or benefits, but about implications. What would happen to autonomy? How would local particularities be respected? Who would control the narrative once a single source of truth existed?

No one voiced those questions aloud.

But everyone was thinking them.

When the first results from the Oracle began to circulate, Olympus grew quieter.

There were no heated arguments. No frontal rejections. Instead, there emerged a series of nuances, doubts, and requests for deeper analysis—reasonable on their own, but together pointing in the same direction: buying time.

The Emperor noticed.

For the first time, he understood that resistance would not take the form of open opposition, but of strategic prudence. No one wanted to block the decision. They wanted to dilute it.

That was when the balance broke.

Not dramatically.

Not in a single meeting.

But through a succession of small gestures that made it clear Olympus was willing to change Emperors before changing the way the Empire saw itself.

Olympus did not eliminate the Emperor out of weakness.

It did so out of internal coherence.

A leader prepared to execute the Oracle's prophecy no longer fit within a council that was not yet ready to live with a shared truth.

The Empire needed stability.

Olympus needed time.

And the Emperor had become a risk.

When the final meeting before his fall ended, no one rose from the table feeling they had made a historic decision. Everything felt normal. Proper. Orderly.

But something had shifted.

Olympus had decided—without saying so—that the Empire should continue operating under the same rules... at least a little longer.

And in that silence, the conflict that would define the future of everything they had built began to take shape.

The Actors of the Empire

No Empire is defined solely by its territories, its systems, or its structures.

It is defined by those who make decisions... and by those who choose not to make them.

This story is not about heroes or villains.

It is about different visions of what it means to govern.

These are the voices that shape the Empire.

Adrián Valcázar
The Emperor

The last leader who attempted to understand the Empire as a single entity.

He inherited a fragmented organization and recognized before many others, that the accumulated debt — technical, operational, and political — could no longer be sustained.

He consulted the Oracle not out of ambition, but out of responsibility.

He paid the price for seeking a shared truth in an Empire that was not yet ready to face it.

Tomás Iriarte
The New Emperor

He arrived after the decision had already been made.

He did not participate in the prophecy, but he inherited its consequences.

His challenge is not technological, but political: deciding whether to execute a transformation he did not help define, or to freeze the future in order to preserve the Empire's immediate stability.

Héctor Salgado
The Librarian

Guardian of the Capital's institutional knowledge.

For years, he sustained the Empire's central system, accumulating experience that does not appear in manuals or contracts.

He seeks neither power nor visibility.

He seeks continuity, scalability, and operational truth.

He understands that an Empire without memory is condemned to repeat its mistakes.

Leonardo Figueroa
The Architect of the Oracle

The voice of objective analysis.

He designed Project Matrix to compare scenarios, not to impose conclusions.

He brings data where there were once speeches.

Scenarios where there were once assumptions.

He knows numbers do not decide on their own…

but he also knows that ignoring them carries an unavoidable cost.

Mateo Krüger
The Sage of the East

He represents the successful past of the Eastern Provinces.

He defends a system that supported that growth for decades.

He does not oppose the Empire as a concept.

He opposes the loss of control over his narrative.

For him, changing the system is not evolution, but the denial of a history that, in his view, still works.

Sebastian Volker
Regent of the Eastern Provinces

He governs the Eastern Provinces with near-absolute autonomy.

He prioritizes speed, local adaptation, and operational independence.

He sees the Empire as a collection of functional territories, not as a unified entity.

His loyalty lies with his provinces, not with the Capital.

Richard "Rick" Coleman
Voice of the Business — Western Provinces

Pragmatic, direct, and operational.

As long as factories produce and customers are served, everything else is secondary.

Global strategy interests him only insofar as it does not interfere with daily operations.

For him, the Empire exists only when it affects production.

Julien Moreau
Voice of the Business — Eastern Provinces

A defender of local efficiency and regional uniqueness.

Each province, in his view, operates under a reality that cannot be measured by common rules.

An imperial system feels to him like a dangerous abstraction.

The plant is real.

The factory exists.

The Empire does not—at least not always.

The Empire is not divided by geography.

It is divided by visions.

And in that tension—between the Capital and the Provinces, between memory and autonomy, between shared truth and local narratives—the impossible decision begins to take shape.

Chapter 3 — The Doctrine of Independence

The doctrine did not begin as a mistake.

It began as a good intention.

After the family stepped away from direct governance, the Empire needed a narrative capable of explaining accelerated growth without disrupting internal harmony. The Capital could not—nor did it want to—become a bottleneck. The Provinces needed room to decide, to adapt, to respond to realities that distance made difficult to fully grasp.

Thus, the doctrine of independence emerged.

It was not written into any statute.

It was not presented as a formal policy.

It simply began to repeat itself—in meetings, in internal communications, in informal conversations: each province must have autonomy to reach its full potential.

For a time, it was unquestionable.

The Capital celebrated results. The Provinces defended their identity. The Empire grew without visible friction. There seemed to be no reason to intervene.

But every doctrine, when left unexamined, eventually turns into dogma.

In the Capital, Héctor Salgado observed the phenomenon with a mixture of respect and concern. As the Empire's Librarian, he understood better than anyone that autonomy without a shared framework has limits. Not out of distrust toward the Provinces, but because of a simpler reality: systems do not scale on goodwill alone.

Every new acquisition brought an exception.

Every exception was justified as temporary.

Every temporary solution became permanent.

Over time, the Empire's Library began to fill with marginal notes—point integrations, customized reports, manual reconciliations, constant efforts to make disparate pieces appear to fit.

It worked.

But at the cost of a complexity no one could see in its entirety.

Héctor knew the problem was not technical.

It was structural.

In the Western Provinces, Rick Coleman did not share those concerns.

To him, the doctrine of independence was common sense. Plants were producing, customers were being served, operational indicators were met. He saw no reason to submit to an imperial vision that, in his experience, usually translated into more controls and less speed.

"As long as they don't stop the line," he liked to say, "they can call it whatever they want."

Rick was not ideological.

He was practical.

For him, the Empire was a distant abstraction. Reality lived on the production floor—in shifts, in deliveries. Any corporate decision that failed to understand that reality was, at best, irrelevant.

In that sense, the doctrine gave him reassurance.

In the Eastern Provinces, independence carried a different meaning.

Julien Moreau viewed it as an acquired right. His territories had been incorporated into the Empire with the implicit promise that their way of operating would be respected. Local systems did more than run daily operations; they represented a way of understanding the business—an identity formed before the Capital even appeared on the map.

For Julien, the doctrine was not a concession.

It was a founding agreement.

"Things are different here," he would repeat. "They always have been."

Spoken with conviction, that phrase closed more debates than it opened.

The problem began when independence ceased to be a tool and became a boundary.

The Eastern Provinces made decisions without considering their impact beyond their borders. Projects designed to solve local problems were launched without regard for replicability. Vendors were selected to meet immediate goals, without an imperial view of continuity.

Sebastian Volker, as Regent of those Provinces, defended that posture with political skill. He did not openly oppose the Empire. He simply prioritized. His decisions responded to regional performance pressures, not to a shared strategy.

"The Capital doesn't understand our urgencies," he would say. "We do."

Within that logic, he was right.

But that logic also carried consequences.

In Olympus, the doctrine of independence functioned as a political buffer. It allowed direct conflict to be avoided. Whenever tension arose, it was enough to remind everyone that the Provinces had autonomy. Debate was postponed. Harmony was preserved.

Mateo Krüger saw in the doctrine a guarantee. To him, it meant the Empire would not erase the past of the Eastern Provinces—that the system that had supported their growth would not be replaced by a solution imposed from the Capital.

"Not everything that grows needs to be unified," he would say calmly. "Sometimes diversity is strength."

No one contradicted him openly.

The Emperor, Adrián Valcázar, began to notice the fracture.

Independence had enabled growth.

But it had also prevented governance.

Every time he attempted to obtain a complete view of the Empire, he encountered different versions of the same reality. Numbers aligned locally, but not always globally. Explanations made sense—within their own frameworks.

There was no bad faith.

There were misaligned incentives.

Adrián understood then that the doctrine had not failed through excess, but through absence: the absence of limits, the absence of a shared framework, the absence of an uncomfortable question—how far can autonomy go without breaking the Empire?

It was within that context that Leonardo Figueroa began to structure the Oracle.

Not as an attack on independence, but as a way to measure its consequences. To compare scenarios. To visualize impacts. To place numbers where there had once been narratives.

Seen through the Oracle, the doctrine revealed something unsettling: the Empire functioned, but it did not understand why. And when something works without being understood, it ceases to be sustainable.

The doctrine of independence was not abolished.

Nor was it openly challenged.

It simply ceased to be sufficient.

The Empire had reached a point where growth required more than good intentions. It required coherence. It required a shared memory. It required accepting that autonomy without alignment is not freedom, but fragmentation.

And for the first time, the Capital dared to articulate the unthinkable:

That perhaps, in order to survive, the Empire would have to redefine what it truly meant to be independent.

Chapter 4 — The Empire's Library

The heart of the Empire was not in Olympus, nor in the Provinces.

It was in the Library.

It was not a physical place, although many believed it was. Nor was it a single system, though almost everyone referred to it as such. The Library was something more complex: the sum of past decisions, accumulated knowledge, and operational experience that sustained the Empire without drawing attention to itself.

Héctor Salgado had spent years walking through its invisible shelves.

As the Librarian, he knew every corridor, every fracture, and every improvised reinforcement that kept the Empire's central structure standing. He knew which parts had been designed with foresight and which had survived through sheer operational discipline.

At the center of the Library lived the Legacy Red System.

It was not new.

It was not elegant.

But it was solid.

It had accompanied the Empire for decades. It had seen plants open and others close, acquisitions absorbed, and crises weathered that no one had ever formally documented. The Red System did not claim modernity, but it offered something the Empire valued more than it liked to admit: predictability.

The Red System was not understood through manuals.

It was understood through practice.

Every adjustment, every development, every correction had been carried out by people who knew the business from the inside. Not intermediaries. Not external vendors bound by temporary contracts. People of the Empire.

That knowledge was not fully written down because it could not be. It was living knowledge—built during night shifts, complex month-end closings, and urgent decisions no one wanted to remember, yet which had saved entire operations.

For Héctor, the Library was not nostalgia.

It was responsibility.

He knew the Red System had limits. He also knew those limits were not immediate, but they were inevitable. The problem was not that the system failed. The problem was that the Empire had grown faster than the architecture that sustained it.

Over time, Héctor came to understand that calling the heart of the Empire a "system" was a dangerous simplification.

The Legacy Red System did not operate alone.

It never had.

Around it, a web of satellite systems had grown—built to address specific needs the core could not meet at the speed operations demanded. Tools connected directly to production machines. Platforms capturing real-time events. Systems that spoke to suppliers, validated materials, recorded incidents, managed quality, and supported decisions that never appeared in executive presentations.

Each of those systems had been born from a legitimate intention: to keep the plant running.

But none had been designed with the Empire as a whole in mind.

Some lived so close to the machines they felt like part of them. Others existed as fragile bridges between suppliers and production. There were solutions no one remembered approving, yet everyone feared shutting down.

The Library was not a book.

It was a network.

And like any network built over time, it had critical nodes known only to a few.

Héctor knew where those sensitive points were. He knew which interface could not be touched during month-end close. Which system must not be restarted during a shift change. Which lost event could trigger a chain of invisible errors.

That knowledge was not in the Red System.

It was in people.

In the Western Provinces, Rick Coleman viewed the Library from afar.

To him, the Red System was simply "the system." It worked. It allowed production, billing, and delivery. He had little interest in how it was built, as long as it did not stand between the plant and the customer.

"If it's still working tomorrow," he would say, "I don't see the problem."

Rick did not dismiss the Library.

He simply did not inhabit it.

The complexity sustaining operations was not part of his daily world. As long as machines kept running and trucks left on time, architecture remained someone else's concern.

In the Eastern Provinces, perception was different.

There, the Library was not the center of the Empire. Each province had built its own. Local systems—adapted, defended, and claimed as part of their identity. Among them stood out the Yellow System, a solution that had grown alongside those regions and had become a symbol of autonomy.

The Yellow System solved local operations quickly. It allowed agile adaptations and offered a sense of immediate control. For Julien Moreau, it represented independence from the Capital.

But it also had limits few wanted to discuss.

It was not designed for an Empire.

It did not think in terms of multiple provinces.

It did not prioritize historical memory or shared traceability.

For Héctor, the problem was not the color.

It was fragmentation.

The Empire's Library worked relentlessly to connect those worlds.

Reconciling data.

Translating definitions.

Unifying reports never meant to coexist.

It worked... but with increasing strain.

Each new integration added complexity. Each local exception demanded further adaptation. The Red System could continue operating, but it could not absorb infinite exceptions without paying a price.

Complexity, when left ungoverned, is not seen.

It is felt.

That was when an uncomfortable idea emerged.

What if the Red System did not need to die... but to evolve?

For a time, that possibility seemed logical. A new generation of the red lineage, more modern, better suited to the Empire's scale. A system that could inherit the Library's knowledge while expanding with the Empire's current size.

Héctor did not reject that option.

He examined it seriously.

But when the Oracle began to model scenarios, it revealed something not everyone expected: evolving red meant continuing to carry past decisions. Improving them, yes, but not fundamentally rethinking them. The satellite ecosystem would remain, with all its dependencies and fragilities.

The Empire did not need stability alone.

It needed future coherence.

In Olympus, the Library was viewed with ambivalence.

Some gods respected it deeply. Others saw it as an anchor. To them, the Red System represented the past, a past that had worked, but one that did not necessarily have to define the future.

Mateo Krüger regarded the Library with distance. He did not dismiss it, but neither did he claim it as his own. For him, the Empire could not be built solely from the Capital. The Eastern Provinces had the right to preserve their way of operating.

"An Empire is not governed by a single book," he would say. "It is governed through local wisdom."

Héctor understood the argument.

But he also knew that too many books without an index inevitably lead to chaos.

The Empire's Library did not seek prominence.

It asked for something simpler:

A conscious decision.

To continue sustaining the Empire on a system that had already given all it could... or to accept that memory would need to be preserved in a different form.

That dilemma was not technical.

It was existential.

And it was at that point that the color Blue began to appear in conversations.

Not as a promise.

Not as an imposition.

But as a possibility no one was yet ready to name.

Chapter 5 — The Inherited System

For years, the Empire had lived under a tacit premise:

If something has worked, it should be able to keep working.

The logic seemed reasonable. It had supported difficult decisions, avoided unnecessary ruptures, and allowed the Empire to grow without visible disruption. No one openly questioned the Legacy Red System, because doing so meant questioning everything that had been built upon it.

The system was not merely a tool.

It was an inheritance.

When the Oracle began to take shape, one of the first questions to surface in Olympus was almost inevitable:

"What if red can still govern?"

It was not nostalgia.

It was prudence.

Evolving the red lineage appeared, at first glance, to be the least risky option. The knowledge already existed. The Library knew it. People understood how to operate it, how to repair it, how to adapt it when something failed. The Empire would not have to learn an entirely new language from scratch.

Héctor Salgado understood that reasoning perfectly.

He himself had raised it quietly long before the conversation reached Olympus.

From the Library, the evaluation of the inherited system was meticulous.

The question was not whether the Red System worked. That had already been answered. The question was more complex: whether it could govern an Empire different from the one that had given it birth.

The Oracle began to model scenarios.

A renewed red.

More modern.

Faster.

Better prepared to scale.

But every scenario carried the same uncomfortable constant: the past did not disappear. It transformed, yes—but it remained present. Decisions made years earlier continued to shape future architecture. Inherited exceptions remained exceptions.

Red could evolve.

But it could not fully reinvent itself.

In the Western Provinces, Rick Coleman viewed the discussion with skepticism.

For him, the question was simple:

"How long would the plant be at risk?"

He had little interest in models or long-term projections. What mattered were immediate impacts. Changing something that worked was always a potential threat to operations.

An evolved red felt acceptable.

A radical change did not.

"If we already know how it works," he would say, "why complicate things?"

Rick was not defending the system.

He was defending continuity.

In the Eastern Provinces, the position was more political.

Julien Moreau and Sebastian Volker saw the evolution of red as an implicit validation of the Capital's Library. Even without open opposition, the idea of the central system becoming the Empire's axis was uncomfortable.

For them, the issue was not technical.

It was control.

A strengthened red could absorb functions that currently lived in local systems. It could standardize processes that had remained flexible. Above all, it could enable direct comparisons.

And comparisons are always unsettling.

Mateo Krüger observed the debate with quiet attention.

From his perspective, evolving red was an elegant way to avoid rupture. It preserved the narrative of continuity without forcing the Eastern Provinces to fully abandon their yellow systems. It was a middle ground—politically defensible.

"Empires do not change at the root," he would say. "They adapt."

No one contradicted him.

But the Oracle did not speak in political terms.

It spoke in structural ones.

As the analysis deepened, it revealed what few wanted to confront: the problem was not only at the core, but in the entire ecosystem surrounding it.

Evolving red also meant:

Rewriting critical interfaces

Redesigning flows connected to production machines

Revalidating supplier events

Retesting integrations never meant to change

Every improvement to the core required revisiting satellites no one wanted to touch.

The inherited system was not a solid block.

It was a network stretched to its limits.

Héctor explained this carefully.

Not as a warning.

As a statement of fact.

"Red can continue to function," he said. "But each year it will cost us more to sustain it. And every new exception will make the system more fragile."

He did not speak of collapse.

He did not speak of disaster.

He spoke of erosion.

And erosion, unlike failure, does not create urgency.

It creates complacency.

The Emperor, Adrián Valcázar, listened in silence.

He knew that evaluating the inherited system was not merely a technological decision. It was a declaration about the kind of Empire they intended to govern. Preserving red, even in an evolved form, meant accepting that the past would continue to define the limits of the future.

That was not necessarily wrong.

But it was a renunciation.

A renunciation of redefining processes.

A renunciation of a common language.

A renunciation of questioning practices designed for a smaller Empire.

The Oracle was clear in its conclusion.

The inherited system could extend the Empire's life.

But it could not transform it.

It was a solution to buy time, not to change direction.

The discussion did not end that day.

No decision was made.

But something had shifted.

For the first time, Olympus understood that the real question was not whether red could continue to govern...

...but how much the Empire was willing to pay for not letting it go.

And in that uncomfortable silence, the idea of the color Blue ceased to be an abstract possibility and became a concrete threat.

Chapter 6 — The Promise of Blue

The color Blue did not appear all at once.

It did not arrive as a formal proposal or a strategic decision. At first, it was little more than a nuance in technical conversations, an indirect reference in comparative analyses, a slide briefly shown and carefully removed.

Blue was not announced.

It was implied.

For the Empire, that made it more dangerous.

Leonardo Figueroa was the first to place it on the table without evasion.

He did not do so in Olympus, nor before everyone. He did it in a technical session—almost intimate—where the Oracle could speak without political filters. There, Blue ceased to be an abstraction and took shape as a different architecture, designed not to inherit the past, but to redefine it.

Blue did not promise continuity.

It promised coherence.

A system designed from the outset to govern large Empires—multiple provinces, shared rules, and a single version of the truth. It did not eliminate business complexity, but it ordered it.

For Leonardo, that distinction changed everything.

Héctor Salgado listened carefully.

As Librarian, he understood better than anyone the hidden cost of that promise. Blue did not merely imply changing a core. It implied redefining the entire Library—deciding which knowledge should migrate, which should be transformed, and which, inevitably, would have to be left behind.

Blue did not preserve memory by default.

It demanded curation.

And curation required difficult decisions.

"Blue is not here to learn how we do things," Héctor thought.

"It is here to tell us how we should do them."

He did not say it aloud.

But he understood it immediately.

In the Western Provinces, the reaction was cautious.

Rick Coleman listened to talk of Blue with the same distrust an operator feels toward a new machine. Not because he doubted its capability, but because he knew every technological promise carries an operational cost.

"How long would it stop us?" he asked.

It was not an ideological objection.

It was an honest question.

Blue spoke of standardized processes, defined flows, integrated controls. All of it sounded reasonable… as long as it did not interrupt production.

For Rick, the promise of Blue made sense only if it could coexist with the reality of the plant floor.

In the Eastern Provinces, the reaction was different.

Julien Moreau saw Blue as a direct threat—not because it was technically inferior, but precisely because it was not. A Blue system, with shared rules and full traceability, would make visible differences that had long been diluted within local narratives.

Blue did not ask.

It compared.

And comparison, in an Empire accustomed to measuring each province by its own rules, was a profoundly political act.

Sebastian Volker understood the risk immediately. He did not express it as open opposition, but began raising strategic questions—costs, timelines, cultural impact, local adaptability.

All were valid.

All pointed in the same direction: buying time.

Mateo Krüger observed Blue's advance with a mixture of skepticism and experience.

He had seen systems promise more than they could deliver. He knew no color could solve an Empire's problems on its own. To him, Blue represented a vision born far from the Eastern Provinces, designed from the logic of the Capital.

"Empires are not governed by theories," he once said. "They are governed by local realities."

He was not wrong.

But he was not complete.

The Oracle, indifferent to political tension, continued to present scenarios.

It compared evolved red with native Blue. It modeled costs, timelines, risks, and benefits. And it revealed something that unsettled even those who defended continuity: Blue did not merely solve the present—it reduced future complexity.

Where red accumulated exceptions, Blue enforced rules.

Where red required translation, Blue spoke a single language.

Where red depended on key individuals, Blue institutionalized knowledge.

It was not perfect.

But it was consistent.

Héctor felt the weight of that consistency.

The promise of Blue was not technical.

It was cultural.

It meant accepting that many historical decisions would need to be revisited. That processes designed to survive would now have to be designed to scale. That autonomy would need to coexist with shared discipline.

Blue did not eliminate the Provinces.

It aligned them.

And that alignment carried an emotional cost the Oracle could not measure.

Adrián Valcázar understood then why Blue generated so much noise.

Not because it was too ambitious.

But because it forced a choice.

A choice between continuing to govern the Empire as a federation of narratives...

or transforming it into a coherent, comparable, and transparent entity.

The promise of Blue was not efficiency.

It was visibility.

And visibility always unsettles those who have learned to operate in the shadows.

The chapter did not close with a decision.

It closed with a certainty.

The Empire could no longer pretend that Blue was merely another option. From that moment on, any path it chose would be measured against that promise.

Red represented continuity.

Blue represented transformation.

And between them, the Empire would have to decide not only which system it wanted...

...but what kind of Empire it was willing to become.

Chapter 7 — The Kingdoms Across the Sea

The Empire did not expand eastward by accident.

The expansion was presented as a strategic victory: new plants, new markets, new productive capabilities. On Olympus's maps, the Eastern Provinces appeared as natural extensions of imperial power, symbols of modernization and global reach.

In reality, they were kingdoms.

The Eastern Territories did not enter the Empire as empty lands. They arrived with history, with established structures, and with identities forged long before becoming part of something larger. Some of those lands had once been Empires in their own right, governed by families who knew every corner of their domain and had survived for years without answering to anyone else.

When they were integrated, they were not conquered.

They were persuaded.

The implicit agreement was simple: they would become part of the Empire, but they would retain their internal rules. The Capital accepted that condition as a gesture of respect, and as the price of rapid growth.

In the early years, the model worked.

The Eastern Provinces grew quickly. They made agile decisions tailored to local markets and delivered results that reinforced the narrative of success. From the Capital, that dynamism was observed with satisfaction, interpreted as proof that operational independence was the key to unlocking each territory's potential.

The Empire was expanding.

And no one wanted to interfere with that momentum.

Over time, that independence ceased to be an exception and became doctrine.

The Eastern Territories developed their own forms of governance, their own rhythms, and their own criteria for success. Imperial policies were interpreted, adapted, or postponed according to local realities, not as open defiance, but as exercises in responsible autonomy.

At least, that was how it was framed.

From within, the logic was clear:

no one understands these kingdoms better than those who govern them.

The relationship with the Capital was always cordial, but distant.

Communication flowed when necessary, not by habit. Time zone differences became a natural argument against deep synchronization. Joint meetings focused on results, not on processes. Each kingdom showed what it chose to show.

And the Capital accepted that dynamic.

Not out of weakness, but out of trust.

Over the years, that trust hardened into custom.

The Eastern Provinces gradually stopped seeing themselves as part of a larger system and began operating as self-sufficient entities, accountable only when circumstances required it. Coordination with the Capital became reactive: when something went wrong, support was requested; when everything worked, the narrative of autonomy was reinforced.

There was never open conflict.

But there was never deep alignment either.

In the East, distance was more than geographic.

Decisions were made through a pragmatic logic, focused on keeping operations running and meeting immediate commitments. Relationships within the Eastern Territories were close; relationships with the Capital were functional. The Empire was a useful umbrella, not a center of governance.

The Eastern Territories, for their part, had built strong identities around their way of doing things. Proprietary processes, trusted vendors, and clear views of what was appropriate for their plants. Any initiative originating from the Capital was evaluated under an unspoken premise: this does not necessarily apply here.

From the Capital, that attitude was not interpreted as resistance.

It was interpreted as maturity.

The idea that each kingdom should reach its full potential without interference became an unquestioned principle. The Empire did not impose; it accompanied. It did not centralize; it trusted. It did not standardize; it respected.

That nobility was celebrated for years.

But every form of nobility carries a cost.

By not insisting on a shared architecture, the Empire allowed the kingdoms across the sea to grow along parallel paths, paths that did not always converge. Paths that, over time, made it harder to understand whether successes were comparable, whether risks were visible, or whether local decisions aligned with a broader vision.

There was no deliberate deception.

There was fragmentation.

The Capital began to feel that fragmentation when projects ceased to be local and began to require real coordination. Integrations that did not fit. Processes that could not be replicated. Decisions always justified by regional context.

Each kingdom was right...

within its own frame.

The Empire was not divided.

But it was not unified either.

And while the kingdoms across the sea continued to govern themselves with pride and autonomy, the Capital began to sense that growth had produced more than expansion, it had produced structural distance.

A distance that was not yet conflict.

But one that would soon demand to be understood.

This chapter does not end with a rupture.

It ends with a silent question that no one in Olympus is yet willing to voice:

Can an Empire be governed in the long term as a collection of independent kingdoms...

or does independence, carried too far, eventually become a boundary?

Chapter 8 — The Local System

In the kingdoms across the sea, the system was not merely a tool.

It was a declaration of identity.

The Eastern Territories did not adopt their local platform by accident or simple convenience. They chose it because it aligned with their way of operating, their pace, and the autonomy they had learned to defend long before becoming part of the Empire. It was not only about functionality; it was about control.

The local system had grown alongside the plants. It adapted to specific processes, regulatory particularities, and practices that, over time, ceased to be questioned. It worked. And when something works, it is rarely asked to explain why.

From the perspective of the kingdoms, the local system represented proximity.

Proximity to users.

Proximity to suppliers.

Proximity to the daily reality of the business.

Decisions were made quickly. Modifications were implemented without long approval cycles. Changes responded to immediate needs, not to long-term plans defined in the Capital.

That pragmatism was seen as a virtue.

The defense of the local system was never technical. Architecture and scalability were rarely discussed. What mattered was experience. The way things had "always been done." How well the provider understood the particularities of the business. How quickly issues were resolved without depending on global agendas.

The local system did not promise a future.

It promised continuity.

And for the kingdoms, that was enough.

In the Eastern Territories, the system became a natural extension of operations.

Each plant had its own instance, its own database, its own universe. Information was not shared by design, but by necessity. When consolidation was required, it was done manually or through specific reports prepared for that purpose.

It was not elegant.

But it worked.

That fragmentation was not perceived as weakness, but as protection. Each kingdom guarded its information as a local asset, not as part of a shared imperial memory.

In some provinces, the logic was similar, though more narrowly focused on operations.

The local system was used to produce, record, and comply. Sophistication was not a priority. Immediate reliability was. Any initiative that put that stability at risk was viewed with caution, regardless of how attractive it appeared on paper.

For many, the system did not need to transform.

It needed not to fail.

From the Capital, the local system was observed with ambivalence.

On one hand, it had undeniably enabled rapid growth. On the other, its design made it difficult to understand the Empire as a whole. Information arrived late, incomplete, or reinterpreted. Comparisons between kingdoms required constant adjustments.

Yet no one openly questioned that model.

Autonomy had been the price of growth.

The narrative in favor of the local system strengthened with each year that passed without a visible crisis. As long as the numbers remained acceptable and the plants continued operating, there was little incentive to rethink the architecture. The local system was not perfect, but it was good enough.

And in Empires, "good enough" often becomes the standard.

The problem was not what the system did.

It was what it was not designed to do.

It had never been conceived to support multiple kingdoms under a single logic. It did not prioritize cross-cutting traceability or data consistency. Each adaptation solved a local problem, but added complexity to the whole.

That complexity remained hidden,

until someone tried to see it from above.

For defenders of the local system, any attempt at change was interpreted as a threat to regional identity. Not as a technical improvement, but as a cultural intrusion. Changing the system meant accepting that the local would have to be subordinated to something larger.

And that was not a technological debate.

It was a debate about power.

The local system endured not because it was the best.

It endured because it belonged.

Because it had accompanied the business for years. Because it knew its shortcuts. Because it responded without questioning. Because it did not demand explanations to a distant authority.

It was comfortable.

It was familiar.

And for that very reason, difficult to challenge.

The Capital had not yet placed the issue explicitly on the table.

But the seed of doubt had already been planted.

As the Empire grew, it became increasingly evident that a collection of local systems could sustain kingdoms,

but not necessarily an Empire.

This chapter does not end with rejection.

It ends with a quiet realization:

The local system had been an effective solution for growth.

But no one had asked whether it was also a solution for governance.

That question still had no answer.

Chapter 9 — Vendors, Not Architects

In the kingdoms across the sea, technology was not governed.

It was contracted.

For years, systems management in the Eastern Territories was built around a simple and seemingly efficient idea: leave complexity in the hands of third parties. Vendors knew the system, understood the business, and responded quickly. For the kingdoms, that was enough.

Architecture was not a concern.

Daily operations were.

The model worked as long as problems remained local.

Each vendor was responsible for its kingdom, its system, and its users. Decisions were made based on immediate urgency, not on design principles. When something failed, it was fixed. When a new need emerged, an adjustment was developed.

There was no malice.

There was pragmatism.

Over time, that pragmatism became habit.

Technology leaders in the kingdoms stopped thinking as designers of the future and began operating as contract administrators. Their value was measured by their ability to obtain fast responses, not by the long-term soundness of the model.

Knowledge resided with the vendors.

Dependency grew quietly.

In the Eastern Territories, the relationship with vendors became almost symbiotic.

They had grown together, solving real problems in specific contexts. The vendor knew the system's shortcuts, the undocumented exceptions, and the particularities that made each plant work. That closeness generated trust, and a dependency that was difficult to acknowledge.

When a strategic question arose, the answer came not from within the kingdom, but from outside.

For them, the model was not a problem to solve. It was a reality that had already proven effective.

Vendors were seen as natural extensions of the local team. They executed, maintained, and adjusted without questioning the overall direction. The priority was not to design a robust system, but to ensure that production did not stop.

Architecture was invisible.

Immediate results were indispensable.

From the Capital, this dynamic was not obvious.

Reports showed stability. Incidents were resolved. Numbers flowed. There were no clear signals of systemic risk. Each kingdom appeared self-sufficient, supported by experts who knew their environment.

The illusion of control was convincing.

But the Empire was not sustained by contracts.

It was sustained by coherence.

And that coherence was beginning to erode.

Each vendor interpreted the system through its own experience. Each local adjustment introduced a variation. Each urgent solution became future debt. There was no shared design, only an accumulation of tactical decisions.

The Empire had no architects.

It had multiple interpreters.

When the Capital attempted to understand the whole, it encountered a mosaic that was difficult to read.

Incomplete documentation. Integrations with no clear owner. Critical processes that worked only because someone knew what to do when something failed. Knowledge was not lost, but it was fragmented.

And fragmentation is not visible,

until one tries to bring things together.

To the kingdoms, this observation seemed exaggerated.

The system worked. Vendors responded. Why question a model that had enabled growth? From their perspective, the Capital was complicating something that was already solved.

The problem was that what was solved locally was not solved at the imperial level.

Vendor dependency was not, by itself, a mistake.

The mistake was confusing support with architecture.

Delegating execution is reasonable. Delegating the design of the future is not. But that boundary had blurred over time, until it disappeared entirely.

The kingdoms had not relinquished control.

They had relinquished the practice of thinking about the system as a whole.

It was in that context that the Capital began to feel a different kind of unease.

This was not about replacing vendors or questioning individual capabilities. It was about understanding whether the Empire still owned its architecture, or whether that responsibility had been ceded without realizing it.

That question could not be answered with contracts.

This chapter does not end with an accusation.

It ends with an uncomfortable realization:

While the kingdoms continued to manage vendors effectively, no one was designing the system the Empire would need tomorrow. Technology was still functioning,

but it had ceased to be strategic.

And when an Empire loses the ability to design its own future, sooner or later it needs an Oracle to reveal what it can no longer see.

Chapter 10 — The Birth of Project Matrix

Project Matrix did not emerge from a visible crisis.

There was no dramatic collapse, no failure that brought the Empire to a halt. Plants continued to produce, systems continued to operate, and reports kept arriving, albeit with delays and qualifications. From the outside, everything appeared to be under control.

But in Olympus, something had changed.

The unease did not arise from a single red number or an isolated event. It emerged from a quiet accumulation of signals: projects that could not be replicated across kingdoms, integrations that worked only where they had been created, and technology decisions consistently justified by local context.

None of this was wrong in isolation.

Taken together, however, it began to form a pattern.

The Empire was growing,

and each layer of growth added complexity.

It was then that the Capital accepted an uncomfortable truth: trusting in the nobility of autonomy was no longer enough. Fragmentation was not a moral failure, it was a structural consequence. And if the Empire intended to endure, it needed to understand what was actually sustaining it.

This was not about changing.

It was about seeing.

The decision to initiate Project Matrix was taken with care.

It was not announced as a systems assessment, nor as a transformation initiative. It was presented as an exercise in deep understanding, a way to map the Empire's technological reality without preconceived judgment.

The name was deliberate.

Matrix evoked structure, connections, and invisible dependencies. It captured the idea that the Empire was sustained by a complex network of accumulated decisions, not by a single central system.

Héctor Salgado was the one who drove the approach.

As Librarian, he knew the Empire's memory was scattered. Documentation, processes, integrations, and institutional knowledge lived across multiple systems and people. Before choosing any path forward, the full map had to be reconstructed.

"We cannot choose a future," he said, "if we do not understand the present."

Olympus accepted that premise.

Project Matrix was founded on a fundamental rule: nothing would be dismissed at the outset.

Not legacy systems.

Not local solutions.

Not current vendors.

Not global alternatives.

Everything would be placed on the table, evaluated under the same criteria, and understood within its real context. The objective was not to assign blame, but to identify patterns.

Unlike previous initiatives, Matrix was not designed from the Capital outward.

It was designed from the plants upward.

Information would not flow only through executive presentations. It would move through real processes, operational walkthroughs, and conversations with those who used the systems every day. The Empire did not want an idealized picture. It wanted an accurate portrait, even if it proved uncomfortable.

It was at this moment that the Oracle began to take shape.

Not as a mystical entity, but as a rigorous methodology capable of absorbing complexity without reducing it to convenience. Matrix did not seek quick answers. It sought shared criteria for comparing different realities.

That ambition, in itself, carried risk.

In the kingdoms across the sea, the news was received with caution.

No one opposed it openly. Official discourse spoke of collaboration and openness. At the same time, legitimate questions emerged. Why evaluate something that works? What problem is being solved? Who will define the criteria?

Autonomy, once granted, is rarely questioned without friction.

In the Capital, Project Matrix was seen as an act of maturity.

It was not about imposing a central solution, but about gaining clarity. The Empire needed a common language to speak about technology, cost, risk, and the future. Without that language, any decision would remain partial.

Matrix did not promise answers.

It promised honesty.

The scope of the project was deliberately broad.

It included central and local systems, machine integrations, financial processes, information flows with suppliers, and human dependencies that were difficult to document. Everything that kept the Empire functioning had to be considered.

Project Matrix would not evaluate tools alone.

It would evaluate ways of governing.

This chapter does not end with a decision.

It ends with a commitment.

The Empire had agreed to submit itself to an unbiased assessment, fully aware that the outcome might unsettle many. From that moment on, the question was no longer whether change would come, but whether the Empire would have the courage to accept what Matrix would reveal.

The Oracle had not yet spoken.

But the Empire had already decided to listen.

Chapter 11 — All Options on the Table

Project Matrix did not begin with a preference.

That was, perhaps, its most uncomfortable characteristic.

From the outset, it was clear that no solution would be protected by history, familiarity, or tradition. The Empire was not seeking to confirm prior intuitions; it was willing to expose itself to an honest evaluation, even if the outcome contradicted years of accumulated decisions.

For the first time, everything was open to discussion.

Héctor Salgado insisted on a condition that many considered unnecessary: no alternative would be dismissed before being fully understood. It did not matter whether a system had been operating for decades or whether another promised absolute modernity. Each option had to be evaluated under the same criteria, without shortcuts or exceptions.

"We are not choosing a tool," he said. "We are choosing a framework of governance."

The distinction mattered.

The first option on the table was the most comfortable one: leaving the Empire as it was.

No change. Maintain the existing systems, strengthen integrations, correct critical points, and accept fragmentation as an inevitable cost of growth. It was the option that generated the least friction and required the fewest explanations.

It was also the option that answered the fewest questions.

Matrix did not discard it.

It evaluated it.

The second option was the evolution of the inherited system.

Extend the Capital's technological core across all kingdoms, modernize it, and adapt it to support the entire Empire. This option carried an obvious advantage: deep internal knowledge, accumulated experience, and a proven history of stability.

It also carried the weight of the past.

The question was not whether it could be done.

It was at what structural cost.

The local system was also placed on the table, without disdain.

It was evaluated not only as a regional solution, but as a potential imperial platform. Its defenders emphasized its agility, its proximity to operations, and its ability to adapt quickly to specific contexts. For some kingdoms, it represented a natural continuity.

Matrix did not judge that position.

It documented it.

The doubt was whether a solution designed for kingdoms could scale without losing coherence when asked to govern an Empire.

Global alternatives were not excluded either.

Platforms designed from their inception to operate across multiple territories, with shared rules and architectures built for complexity. These options promised consistency, traceability, and a unified view of the business.

They also implied profound change.

Adopting them was not merely a systems implementation.

It meant accepting a new way of operating.

Héctor was clear from the beginning: Matrix would not evaluate isolated promises.

Each option would be analyzed through real imperial scenarios. Financial processes, industrial operations, machine integrations, supplier relationships, and human dependencies would all be part of the assessment. Nothing would be excluded for the sake of comfort.

The objective was not to find the perfect option.

It was to understand the sacrifices each path required.

In the kingdoms across the sea, this breadth generated unease.

Some interpreted the evaluation as a veiled threat. Others saw it as an opportunity to prove that local solutions were sufficient. In any case, the message was unmistakable: the Empire would no longer accept decisions based solely on custom.

Matrix's neutrality was unsettling.

In the Capital, the discussion took on a different tone.

Placing all options on the table meant accepting that none were guaranteed. Neither the inherited system, nor local solutions, nor global platforms could be assumed to be predetermined winners.

For the first time, technology ceased to be a matter of trust and became a matter of explicit comparison.

Project Matrix advanced without early conclusions.

No rankings were published. No preferences were leaked. Each alternative continued its path, accumulating evidence, strengths, and limitations. The decision was still distant.

But something had already changed.

The Empire had accepted that choosing meant renouncing.

And that no renunciation would be trivial.

This chapter does not offer answers.

It offers legitimacy.

When the Oracle spoke, no one would be able to claim they had not been heard. All options had been given space, time, and clear criteria. The decision, whatever it might be, would be supported by a process that did not hide behind tradition or urgency.

The Empire had opened the entire board.

Now all that remained was to walk the labyrinth that such openness had created.

Chapter 12 — Giants and Specialists

Once the board was fully open, Project Matrix revealed an unavoidable tension.

This was not a debate between "good" and "bad" systems.

It was a debate between scale and specialization.

The giants arrived with promises of global coherence.

The specialists arrived with deep mastery of the craft.

And the Empire needed both.

The giants spoke the language of the Empire.

Their architectures were designed to operate across multiple territories under shared rules. They offered end-to-end traceability, a single data model, and processes built to coexist with regulatory, fiscal, and operational complexity. They did not improvise; they standardized.

In their presentations, the Empire appeared ordered.

The Provinces aligned.

Information comparable.

The promise was clear: visibility without translation.

The giants, however, were not naive.

They understood that their strength was also their constraint. To operate, they required discipline. To scale, they demanded renunciation. They did not adapt to every exception; they turned it into a rule or eliminated it altogether.

Adopting them meant accepting that the Empire itself would have to change, not only the system.

The specialists, by contrast, spoke the language of the workshop.

They knew the industry, the production cycles, the particularities of casting, machining, and assembly. Their solutions were finely tuned to solve concrete problems with surgical precision. Where the giants proposed frameworks, the specialists offered expert shortcuts.

For many plants, that proximity was irreplaceable.

The specialists did not promise Empires.

They promised local efficiency.

Their systems excelled in specific processes: production planning, quality control, lot-level traceability, direct machine integration. They were fast, flexible, and deeply adapted to the business.

That same specialization, however, made them difficult to integrate into a shared vision.

Each solution resolved a problem, and introduced another at the collective level.

Project Matrix favored neither side.

It placed giants and specialists before the same scenarios. It evaluated not their narratives, but their behavior: how they responded to real imperial processes, how they coexisted with existing systems, how they handled exceptions without breaking coherence.

The contrast was revealing.

The giants absorbed complexity.

Not always elegantly, but consistently. Where they encountered an exception, they asked for the rule. Where a process was unique, they sought to standardize it. Their approach was systemic.

The specialists solved problems quickly.

Where there was friction, they offered immediate solutions. Where a process did not fit, they adjusted it. Their approach was tactical, oriented toward local results.

Both were valid.

But they were not equivalent.

For the kingdoms across the sea, specialists felt more familiar.

They spoke their language, understood their rhythm, and did not challenge autonomy. The giants, by contrast, were perceived as foreign structures, designed far from the daily reality of the plants.

The resistance was not technical.

It was cultural.

From the Capital, the reading was different.

Specialists solved problems, but they did not build governance. Each new solution added an integration point, another dependency, another piece to the puzzle. The question was not whether they worked, but whether they could coexist without fragmenting the whole.

The Empire needed more than isolated efficiency.

It needed coherence.

Project Matrix documented these tensions without judgment.

It did not seek to declare premature winners. It sought to understand the cost of each choice. Choosing the giants meant sacrificing local flexibility. Choosing the specialists meant accepting growing complexity.

There was no path without trade-offs.

This chapter does not exclude anyone.

But it introduces a fundamental truth:

Not all systems are designed for the same purpose.

Some are built to master the complexity of an Empire.

Others are built to perfect the execution of a craft.

Confusing those purposes is the first mistake of any transformation.

Project Matrix moved forward with that clarity.

The decision would not be between brands or promises, but between models of governance. And that decision, still distant, would demand renunciations that no provider could assume on behalf of the Empire.

Chapter 13 — When the Smaller Ones Step Away

Not every exclusion is a defeat.

Within Project Matrix, some occurred without confrontation, without formal announcements, and without the need to justify painful decisions. They simply happened when reality was placed directly against existing limits.

The smaller players were the first to understand it.

From the beginning, Matrix made one thing clear: this would not be a symbolic evaluation. The scenarios were real, the processes complete, and the expectations explicit. The task was not to demonstrate isolated capabilities, but to sustain the Empire as a whole.

For some participants, that scale was revealing.

The smaller solutions arrived with enthusiasm.

They demonstrated agility, deep knowledge of specific processes, and a closeness to daily operations that was undeniably attractive. In local contexts, their proposals were solid. In limited environments, even exceptional.

But when they were asked to look beyond the kingdom, the silence began to carry weight.

The Empire was not demanding omnipotence.

It was demanding coherence.

The smaller players quickly understood that they were not being asked to cover every front, but to coexist with them. To integrate with existing systems, respect shared rules, and scale without losing traceability. For many, that would have required becoming something they were not.

And they were not willing to do so.

The withdrawal was not forced.

It was honest.

Some acknowledged that their strength lay precisely in not becoming giants. Others accepted that their offerings shone in specific contexts, not within imperial structures. Continuing would have meant promising what they could not sustain.

Project Matrix valued that clarity.

For the Empire, these exits were a positive signal.

They confirmed that the process was working. There were no favorites and no predetermined paths. The evaluation did not expel; it revealed. And revealing limits was as valuable as demonstrating strengths.

From the kingdoms across the sea, the withdrawals were observed with a mixture of relief and skepticism.

Relief, because the noise diminished.

Skepticism, because the board began to tilt toward more structured solutions, less flexible, less "local."

The evaluation was starting to feel real.

In the Capital, the message was different.

Each withdrawal confirmed that the decision would not be trivial. The remaining options implied deep commitments. The discussion was no longer about choosing among many paths, but about accepting the consequences of the few that remained.

Matrix moved forward, and the margin for ambiguity narrowed.

This chapter does not celebrate a victory.

It acknowledges a necessary honesty.

The smaller players were not excluded due to technical insufficiency, but due to strategic fit. They recognized that the Empire required something different from what they could offer, and they had the maturity to say so before forcing a narrative.

Not every project allows for such a dignified exit.

Matrix did.

When the smaller ones stepped away, Project Matrix entered a new phase.

The evaluation ceased to be exploratory and began to turn decisive. The remaining options could no longer hide behind promises. They would have to demonstrate not only that they worked, but that they could sustain the Empire without fragmenting it.

The labyrinth was narrowing.

Chapter 14 — Specialized Systems

Not all specialists were small.

Some had been born at the very heart of the industry, shaped by decades of direct contact with furnaces, machining centers, and assembly lines. Their systems did not speak in abstractions. They spoke in metal, tolerances, and cycle times.

For many plants within the Empire, these solutions were synonymous with operational excellence.

These systems knew the craft.

They understood how to plan a melt, how to balance a line, how to trace a defective batch back to its exact origin. They integrated machine data, sensors, and quality controls with a natural ease that the giants often envied.

On the shop floor, they excelled.

They did not promise governance.

They promised precision.

For the kingdoms across the sea, these platforms represented the best of both worlds.

They were more robust than local systems and closer to operations than imperial giants. They had been designed for the automotive industry, understood the pressure of Tier 1 and Tier 2 customers, and responded quickly to shifts in demand.

From their perspective, what more could the Empire need?

Project Matrix did not dismiss that question.

On the contrary, it pushed it to its limits.

Each specialized system was subjected to real scenarios: multiple plants, distinct legal entities, currencies, fiscal regulations, and interconnected supply chains. The evaluation was not about running a single plant, but about coordinating many without losing coherence.

That is where the tensions emerged.

Specialized systems were deep, but narrow.

Their strength lay in mastering specific production processes. When asked to extend that logic to complex finance, global consolidations, or imperial reporting, they required extensions, integrations, or parallel developments.

Each adjustment solved one case, and added complexity to the whole.

For the Empire, that complexity was not invisible.

Each specialized system introduced a new integration point, an additional dependency, and another layer of interpretation. The global view fractured into multiple partial perspectives that had to be reconciled manually.

The question was no longer whether they could operate.

It was whether they could govern.

From the Capital, the dilemma became clear.

An industrial Empire needs operational excellence, but it also needs financial consistency, cross-enterprise traceability, and a shared narrative. Specialized systems answered the question of how to produce, but not always how to explain or how to compare.

The Empire could not live on the shop floor alone.

For the kingdoms, this observation felt distant.

In their daily reality, production was central. As long as machines ran and customers were satisfied, the system fulfilled its purpose. Global architecture felt like a conceptual luxury, far removed from the pressure of the plant floor.

The distance between these visions was real.

Project Matrix documented that gap without dramatizing it.

It acknowledged the undeniable value of specialized systems in demanding industrial contexts. It also recognized that, when elevated to the imperial level, their local strength became structural fragmentation.

This was not a design flaw.

It was a consequence of their original purpose.

This chapter does not discredit specialists.

It places them where they naturally belong.

Some systems are born to master critical processes with precision. Others are built to articulate broad visions. Forcing one to assume the role of the other does not create excellence. It creates tension.

The Empire was beginning to understand that choosing did not mean denying industry, but deciding from where it would be governed.

With this clarity, Project Matrix moved into a more demanding phase.

The remaining options could no longer hide behind technical strength alone. They would have to demonstrate that they could sustain both the operation and the imperial truth at the same time.

The labyrinth continued to narrow.

Chapter 15 — The Illusion of the Perfect Matrix

As Project Matrix advanced, the Empire began to feel comfortable.

Too comfortable.

The options had been identified, the smaller players had withdrawn, and the specialists had revealed both their strengths and their limits. Only a few alternatives remained on the table, yet the process continued to feel rigorous, orderly, and above all, measurable.

It was the perfect moment to turn complexity into numbers.

Matrices began to multiply.

Rows of criteria, columns of systems, carefully debated weightings. Functionality, scalability, cost, risk, vendor dependency, user experience, integration capability. Every dimension found its place in a table.

At last, the Empire seemed to have a way to compare the incomparable.

From Olympus, the matrices brought reassurance.

They reduced long debates to percentages. They transformed opinions into scores. They allowed the decision to be observed from a safe distance, without entering the noise of operational detail.

The matrix did not argue.

The matrix showed.

In the kingdoms, the matrices were met with skepticism.

Some saw them as excessive simplification. Others as an inevitable formality. For many, they failed to capture the reality of the shop floor or the daily pressure of producing without failure.

"Numbers do not understand the business," some murmured.

And they were not entirely wrong.

Project Matrix did not reject the criticism.

It absorbed it.

Héctor was explicit. Matrices were not meant to decide. They were meant to support thinking. They were tools to organize the conversation, not substitutes for judgment. Every score required an explanation. Every difference required context.

Without that discipline, the matrix would become a mirage.

Even so, the temptation was strong.

Seeing one option stand out by a few decimal points created a false sense of absolute objectivity. It seemed as though the Empire could delegate the decision to a formula, freeing itself from the political and cultural weight that any choice would inevitably carry.

The matrix promised neutrality.

But it concealed prior choices.

Because no matrix is innocent.

Criteria reflect values.

Weightings reflect priorities.

Scales reflect interpretation.

What is chosen to be measured defines what matters. And what does not fit into the table risks disappearing from the debate, even if it is crucial to the future of the Empire.

In some exercises, the differences were minimal.

Tenths separating one system from another. Percentages that, outside their context, appeared decisive. In those moments, the discussion intensified rather than diminished. Every point was defended as if it represented an absolute truth.

The matrix, designed to bring order, began to create tension.

Héctor intervened when the process threatened to lose its purpose.

"If we believe the matrix decides for us," he warned, "we have already failed. The matrix does not see power, it does not see culture, it does not see fear. It only sees what we ask it to see."

The silence that followed was uncomfortable.

The Empire understood then that the perfect matrix did not exist.

Not because the numbers were wrong, but because the reality they attempted to capture was more complex than any model. Matrices were useful, but incomplete. They structured the conversation, but they did not close it.

The decision would remain human.

This chapter does not invalidate the method.

It humanizes it.

Project Matrix continued to use matrices, but with a different awareness. No longer as final judges, but as partial mirrors. The decision was approaching, along with the recognition that no number would shield the Empire from the consequences.

The illusion of the perfect matrix slowly dissolved.

In its place remained a more uncomfortable, but more honest certainty. Choosing would require responsibility. No formula would absorb the political, cultural, and human impact of the decision.

The Oracle was drawing closer to speaking.

And when it did, no one would be able to hide behind a table.

Chapter 16 — The Fear of Transparency

No one in the Empire openly said they were afraid.

Fear was not a word used in Olympus or in the Provinces. It was disguised as prudence, as financial responsibility, as respect for local particularities. It presented itself as legitimate concern for operational impact or as a defense of culture.

But it was fear.

The Blue option did not threaten failure.

It threatened exposure.

For years, the Empire had learned to live with multiple truths. Not false ones, but partial ones. Each province reported from its own reality, using its own rules, its own timing, and its own explanations. Numbers were consolidated, but the stories did not always align.

That had been sufficient as long as growth continued.

Total transparency was not necessary when no one asked too many questions.

When the Oracle modeled the Blue scenario, it introduced an idea that was unsettling from the very beginning, a single version of the truth.

A single financial language.

A single operational model.

A single record of events.

None of that sounded threatening in theory. In practice, it implied something far deeper, the end of explaining results through context and the beginning of comparing them without nuance.

Transparency did not accuse.

It compared.

And comparison strips away the layers that narratives tend to soften.

In the Western Provinces, Rick Coleman did not feel attacked, but he did feel uneasy.

For him, absolute transparency was a potential distraction. He knew that every plant had its particularities, its constraints, its tactical decisions. He feared that a common system would fail to distinguish between a well managed exception and an operational mistake.

"Not everything can be measured the same way," he said. "Not everything can be compared."

Rick was not defending opacity.

He was defending room to maneuver.

Even so, he understood that Blue was not designed to punish. It was designed to align. Still, the idea that someone in the Capital could see his operation with the same level of detail that he himself saw it was uncomfortable.

In the Eastern Provinces, the fear was denser.

Julien Moreau understood from the outset what imperial transparency implied, not only operationally, but financially. A Blue system would make visible relationships that had previously dissolved into local structures. Revenues, costs, external support, apparent efficiencies.

Nothing illegal.

Nothing explicitly wrong.

But not fully comparable either.

Transparency did not judge intentions.

It displayed results without political context.

And that could change conversations in Olympus.

Sebastian Volker was more cautious.

He did not speak of fear.

He spoke of cultural impact.

He outlined scenarios in which transparency could generate unnecessary friction between Provinces. Where direct comparison could erode trust. Where the Capital, armed with detailed data, might be tempted to intervene more than necessary.

"An Empire that is too visible," he said, "risks governing through numbers rather than reality."

The argument was sophisticated.

And partially true.

But it also avoided an uncomfortable question. What happens when reality does not withstand comparison?

Mateo Krüger observed how the debate shifted.

The discussion was no longer about implementation costs.

Nor deployment timelines.

Nor even technical risks.

It was about governance.

For him, absolute transparency represented a rupture with the founding spirit of the Eastern Provinces. An Empire that could see everything was an Empire that could decide everything. From his perspective, that broke the original balance.

"Trust is not built through surveillance," he said in Olympus. "It is built through respect."

No one contradicted him.

Héctor Salgado listened with mixed emotions.

As Librarian, he knew transparency was not the enemy. It was the natural consequence of a coherent system. Without it, the Empire would continue to depend on key individuals to interpret fragmented data.

But he also understood the fear. He had seen how a poorly understood number could lead to the wrong decision. He knew that showing without explaining could be as dangerous as hiding.

Transparency required institutional maturity.

Not just technology.

Leonardo Figueroa, for his part, did not speak of fear.

He spoke of inevitability.

The Oracle did not take sides, but it revealed clear patterns. Empires that avoided transparency gained time, not sustainability. Those that embraced it suffered initial friction, but reduced structural conflict over the long term.

"The problem is not seeing," he said. "The problem is not being ready for what you see."

Adrián Valcázar understood the true dilemma then.

The fear of transparency was not fear of a system.

It was fear of losing narrative control.

For years, each province had told its story in its own words. Blue proposed a shared story, written with shared data. It did not erase particularities, but it made them visible within a common frame.

That changed power.

The Empire was not facing a technological decision.

It was facing an ethical one.

Accepting transparency meant accepting that some truths would no longer be negotiable. That certain results could no longer be explained solely through context. That Olympus would have to govern with comparable information, not carefully balanced narratives.

Fear did not stop the discussion.

But it slowed it.

And in that calculated delay, the Empire began to understand that the impossible decision was not choosing between Red and Blue.

It was deciding how much truth it was willing to bear.

Chapter 17 — The Price of Change

After transparency, cost always arrives before the decision.

It does not arrive as a definitive number or a clear answer, but as an uncomfortable question repeated in different voices: how much will it cost?

In the Empire, that question was not naïve. It had been asked too many times to justify postponements, partial adjustments, and intermediate solutions. But now, facing Blue, the question carried a different weight.

Because this time, cost could not be diluted over time. It was the inevitable consequence of transparency.

Leonardo Figueroa presented the scenarios with surgical precision.

He did not speak of "implementation."

He spoke of transformation.

He showed that the cost of Blue was not limited to licenses, services, or infrastructure. Those were the visible numbers, the ones that could be discussed and negotiated. The real cost lay elsewhere, redesigning processes, training people, stopping inertia.

Blue did not adapt to the Empire.

It required the Empire to adapt to it.

That had a price.

In the Capital, the first figures produced silence.

Not because they were impossible, but because they were explicit. The inherited Red system had always allowed costs to be hidden in incremental maintenance, in isolated developments, in temporary solutions that became permanent without formal approval.

Blue did not work that way.

Every decision had a clear impact.

Every phase had a defined budget.

Every delay had a visible consequence.

Transparency made cost unavoidable.

Héctor Salgado looked at the numbers with a mixture of realism and resignation.

He knew the cost of change was not only financial. It was human. Every satellite system that had to be reconfigured meant difficult conversations. Every integration that had to disappear meant admitting that a historical solution was no longer sustainable.

Change would touch people.

And people rarely appear clearly in budgets.

"The real cost," he thought, "is not in the final number, but in the daily friction over years."

He did not say it out loud.

But he knew it.

In the Western Provinces, Rick Coleman reacted with relentless logic.

"How many plant hours?" he asked. "How many weekends? How many false starts?"

Total figures meant little to him if they could not be translated into operational impact. For Rick, every hour devoted to change was an hour not producing. Every training session was a shift less focused on delivery.

Rick did not oppose change.

He opposed losing focus.

Cost, from his perspective, was risk.

In the Eastern Provinces, cost took on a different meaning.

Julien Moreau saw in Blue's numbers a double threat. Not only because they implied investment, but because they made comparison inevitable. The cost of change would be measured against historical results, and any difference would be interpreted as efficiency or inefficiency.

Sebastian Volker reinforced that concern with strategic arguments, cultural impact, local resistance, loss of flexibility. He argued that cost could not be evaluated solely from the Capital, but from each province.

"The same change has different prices depending on where it is paid," he said.

He was right.

But the Empire needed a common reference.

Mateo Krüger observed the discussion from another angle.

For him, the cost of change should not be measured only in investment, but in rupture. Changing systems meant breaking with a way of operating that had been successful for decades. That carried a symbolic cost no spreadsheet could capture.

"Empires that forget their history," he warned, "pay a price that is not always visible immediately."

He was not speaking of money.

He was speaking of identity.

The Oracle, indifferent to emotional weight, continued to present scenarios.

It compared the accumulated cost of sustaining Red over ten years with the initial cost of Blue. It showed how incremental maintenance turned into debt. How every exception created more dependency. How the invisible cost of the past eventually surpassed the explicit cost of change.

It was not an ideological argument.

It was arithmetic.

But arithmetic, when it challenges beliefs, generates resistance.

Adrián Valcázar then understood the true nature of the dilemma.

The Empire was not debating whether it could afford the change.

It was debating when it would pay for it.

Pay now, with concentrated pain and full visibility.

Or pay later, in invisible installments that would erode the ability to decide.

The cost of change was not a surprise.

It was a choice.

The silence that followed that realization was not uncomfortable.

It was heavy.

Because everyone understood that, from that moment on, not deciding also had a price. Every month without definition added hidden costs. Every local project approved outside the imperial framework made any future decision more expensive.

Change did not wait.

It only accumulated interest.

The chapter did not close with an agreement.

It closed with a shared certainty, unspoken but understood. The Empire was already paying the cost.

It simply had not yet wanted to see it reflected in a single number.

And in that tacit recognition, Project Matrix ceased to be an evaluation exercise and became a point of no return.

Chapter 18 — Extraordinary Revenue

Transparency does not arrive all at once.

It arrives in layers.

First, it organizes.

Then, it compares.

And finally, it reveals.

When the Oracle began consolidating information under a single language, the Empire did not immediately see anomalies. The numbers still reconciled. The reports still made sense. Nothing appeared out of place.

Until a new category emerged.

It did not appear as an error.

Nor as a deviation.

It appeared as a footnote, a line that had never been relevant before because it had never been comparable: extraordinary revenue.

The term raised no alarm in the Olympus. It was familiar, accepted, even reasonable. Subsidies, temporary support, regional incentives. Nothing unusual for an Empire operating across multiple territories.

What was extraordinary was not its existence.

It was its weight.

When the data was observed as a whole, something caught the Oracle's attention.

In some Eastern Provinces, extraordinary revenue was not marginal. It had shifted from being an occasional supplement to becoming a meaningful component of results. It did not dominate the narrative, but it tilted it.

This was not obvious at first glance.

It only appeared through comparison.

For years, those revenues had coexisted with operations without conflict. While they existed, they helped offset inefficiencies, sustain margins, and soften difficult decisions. No one hid them. They were simply absorbed into the financial story without much scrutiny.

The problem emerged when they disappeared.

The Oracle identified a troubling pattern.

At the moment the support ended, two Eastern Provinces posted negative results for the first time in years. There was no dramatic collapse, only a quiet correction. What had once looked like stability revealed its fragility.

Profitability had not vanished.

It had been inflated.

No one spoke of deception.

There was no need to.

The numbers were accurate. The records were valid. But the story they told had changed. True operating profitability was lower than the Empire had believed, and the difference was not tied to performance, but to external and temporary factors.

Transparency did not accuse.

It simply removed the scaffolding.

In the Olympus, the discussion grew tense.

Not because of the past, but because of the future. If extraordinary revenue had been structurally embedded in results, what did that mean for strategic decisions made on those figures? How many projects had been approved under a distorted perception of strength?

The questions did not seek blame.

They sought lost context.

From the Eastern Provinces, the response was measured, but defensive.

Subsidies were legitimate. They were part of the economic environment of the time. No one could have predicted their disappearance. All of this was true. But none of it answered the central concern: why had those revenues been treated as normal?

The answer was not explicit.

It was cultural.

For years, each Province had told its story in the way that best explained its results. As long as there was no direct comparison, that narrative was sufficient. The Empire trusted the story because it had no other way to see.

Transparency changed that.

For the first time, results were observed without the filter of local exception. Profit was no longer explained by context, but by structure.

Héctor then understood the true impact of the finding.

This was not an accounting issue.

It was a governance issue.

An Empire that makes strategic decisions must distinguish between operating performance and temporary circumstances. Without that distinction, growth rests on unstable ground.

The Oracle was not pointing out errors.

It was revealing invisible risks.

Leonardo was more direct.

"If we cannot separate what is extraordinary from what is recurring," he said, "we are governing blind."

No one disagreed.

Because once seen, the numbers could not be unseen.

This chapter does not end with an accusation or a crisis.

It ends with a lingering discomfort.

The Empire understood that transparency did not only reveal operational differences, but also narrative dependencies. Some Provinces were not less capable, but they had been sustained by factors that no longer existed.

And that truth, once exposed, demanded a response.

Extraordinary revenue ceased to be a technical detail.

It became a mirror.

And before that mirror, the Empire began to understand why the impossible decision was not technological, but profoundly political.

Chapter 19 — The Fear of a Single Ledger

Fear rarely presents itself as resistance.

Sometimes, it presents itself as technical caution.

When the idea of a single ledger began to take shape within Project Matrix, it was not operations that raised the first concerns. It was the consolidation teams, those responsible for transforming local realities into a financial truth the Olympus could understand.

Their concern was not ideological.

It was accounting.

A single ledger sounded, in theory, like clarity.

One record of events.

One source of data.

One financial narrative.

But for those who lived in the world of consolidation, the proposal opened an uncomfortable question: how would such unification coexist with the rules the Empire was required to respect beyond itself?

IFRS was not a suggestion.

It was an obligation.

For years, consolidation had functioned as an act of translation. Each Province recorded its reality according to its own particularities. Then, the Capital adjusted, reclassified, and harmonized to comply with international standards. It was not perfect, but it was familiar. The process absorbed differences without forcing them to disappear.

A single ledger threatened to remove that buffer zone.

"Consolidation is not addition," they explained. "It is interpretation."

IFRS rules did not always align with local operational logic. They required adjustments, eliminations, reclassifications, and professional judgment. Centralizing the recording of transactions could facilitate comparison, yes, but it could also rigidify processes that required regulatory flexibility.

The fear was not loss of control.

It was loss of compliance capacity.

The Oracle listened carefully to these concerns.

It did not dismiss them as resistance to change. It acknowledged that a single ledger could not be naïve. If transparency was meant to strengthen the Empire, it could not do so at the expense of violating the rules that legitimized it before the world.

Transparency without compliance was merely exposure.

Héctor insisted on separating concepts that were becoming dangerously intertwined.

A single ledger did not mean a single accounting criterion without nuance. It meant a common origin of information, upon which the necessary interpretations could be applied to comply with IFRS.

The problem was not technical.

It was trust in the design.

From the Provinces, the concern took on a different tone.

A single ledger implied that adjustments would no longer be made "at the end," but would need to be discussed "at the beginning." Accounting decisions could no longer be resolved at the boundary between Province and Capital. They would become visible from the source.

That was not merely a process change.

It was a shift in power.

Leonardo observed as the debate became entangled.

Some feared that the rigidity of a single ledger would suffocate operations. Others feared that the flexibility required by IFRS would reintroduce the very fragmentation Matrix sought to eliminate. The tension was not contradictory. It was inherent to any Empire attempting to be both transparent and compliant at the same time.

There were no simple solutions.

The fear of a single ledger was not fear of standards.

It was fear of early exposure.

Under the previous model, many decisions were adjusted far from collective view. The new approach required criteria to be visible from the outset. Differences had to be explained before consolidation, not after.

That forced the Empire to mature conversations it had postponed for years.

Adrián understood this with political clarity.

"A single ledger does not eliminate complexity," he said. "It brings it forward."

And bringing it forward meant confronting questions the Empire had long avoided: what is recurring, what is exceptional, what is operational, and what is financial. IFRS demanded clear answers to these questions, and a single ledger would no longer allow them to be buried in late adjustments.

This chapter does not demonize consolidation.

It dignifies it.

It recognizes that the fear did not stem from opacity, but from responsibility. Consolidation teams did not fear transparency. They feared that a poor implementation would confuse clarity with oversimplification.

Mature transparency does not eliminate professional judgment.

It makes it visible.

In the end, the Empire understood that the dilemma was not choosing between a single ledger and IFRS.

It was designing a system capable of sustaining both.

A common data origin, rigorous interpretation, and governance strong enough to explain differences without hiding them. The decision would not be easy, but the alternative, continuing to translate fragmented realities, was no longer sustainable.

The fear of a single ledger did not stop Project Matrix.

But it made one thing unmistakably clear: transparency is not achieved by imposing uniformity, but by building trust that the system can reveal the truth and comply with the rules that give that truth legitimacy.

The Empire moved forward.

It now knew that the impossible decision would not be resolved through technology, but through institutional design.

Chapter 20 — The Oracle Speaks

The Oracle was not born in a boardroom.

It was born in the Library.

It was Héctor Salgado, the Librarian of the Empire, who understood from the beginning that no decision would carry legitimacy unless it was built upon a complete truth. Comparing systems in abstraction was not enough, nor was listening to vendors skilled at selling ideal futures. The Empire needed to look at itself without filters.

"If we are going to decide," he said, "we will decide with everything on the table."

That was the condition.

Héctor did not delegate the evaluation.

He orchestrated it.

The Oracle did not feed solely on documents, presentations, or evaluation matrices. It went to the plants. It crossed the Provinces of the West and the East. It observed real processes, not diagrams. It listened to those who operated the Legacy Red System, those who defended the Yellow System, and those who kept alive the satellite systems no one mentioned in Olympus.

Nothing was discarded at the outset.

Nothing was taken for granted.

Every flow was reviewed.

Every integration was questioned.

Every exception was understood in its context.

The evaluation was not seeking culprits.

It was seeking reality.

In every plant, the Oracle spoke with operators, supervisors, engineers, and system owners. People who never attended strategic meetings, yet knew the Empire better than many gods of Olympus.

Uncomfortable truths emerged.

Processes that functioned thanks to undocumented manual interventions. Satellite systems sustaining critical events without formal ownership. Interfaces no one dared to touch because "they had always been there."

The Oracle did not judge.

It recorded.

Héctor knew that this information was fragile. Exposing it without context could generate resistance. But he also knew that without it, any recommendation would be incomplete.

The Oracle's legitimacy depended on having listened to everyone.

Leonardo Figueroa fulfilled his role with precision.

He did not lead the evaluation.

He structured it.

He took the information Héctor gathered and transformed it into comparable scenarios. He designed clear, weighted, and transparent criteria. He did not erase nuance, but he ordered it. The Oracle did not reduce reality. It made it legible.

Each alternative was evaluated with the same rigor:

Continue as the Empire was

Evolve the Red System

Consolidate the Yellow System

Transform the Empire with the Blue System

There were no shortcuts.

The Legacy Red System was analyzed deeply. Not only for its stability, but for its ability to absorb processes it had never been designed to support. The Oracle spoke with those who operated it, those who defended it, and those who patched it when something failed.

Red remained reliable.

But its reliability depended increasingly on key individuals.

The Oracle identified an uncomfortable truth: Red did not fail because it was perfect, but because it was known. And that knowledge was not easily transferable.

Evolving it was possible.

Freeing it from its past was not.

The Yellow System was heard with the same respect.

Its operators, defenders, and local adaptors were all consulted. No one denied its agility or its closeness to operations. But when the Oracle attempted to project it at an imperial scale, its limitations appeared without exaggeration.

Yellow had not been designed to coexist with other kingdoms.

It did not offer a shared memory.

It did not guarantee cross-territorial traceability.

It worked where it was born.

Not where it would need to govern.

Its exclusion was not a rejection.

It was an acknowledgment of limits.

The option of not changing was also evaluated seriously.

The Oracle treated it as a legitimate alternative, not an omission. It modeled the Empire's future if the current state remained unchanged: more integrations, more exceptions, greater dependence on key individuals.

Not changing was not free.

It was simply silent.

The numbers revealed something difficult to dispute: over the medium term, the accumulated cost of inertia exceeded any initial investment. Technical debt did not stabilize. It grew.

Staying the same was not preservation.

It was postponement.

The Blue System was evaluated without indulgence.

It was not assumed to be superior.

It was required to prove it.

Its implementers passed through strict filters. Some understood the theory but not the industry. Others understood the technology but not the cultural complexity of the Empire. Several were eliminated in the process.

The Oracle was not looking for promises.

It was looking for consistency.

When Blue was tested against the real processes observed in the plants, something shifted. For the first time, a system did not require constant translation. The language was common. The rules were explicit. Traceability was inherent.

It did not eliminate complexity.

It organized it.

When the time came to consolidate results, no one expected a decisive answer.

And none came.

Evolved Red was close.

Blue was close.

The differences were minimal, measured in tenths rather than whole points. Tenths in critical functionality. Tenths in technical architecture. Tenths in the ability to absorb future growth without multiplying exceptions.

In cost, Blue was not the cheapest option.

But neither was it the most expensive when the full horizon was considered.

The Oracle did not choose out of enthusiasm.

It chose out of structural balance.

Héctor Salgado presented the conclusion.

Not as a victory.

As a responsibility.

He explained that the Oracle was not declaring the past incorrect. It was stating that the future demanded a different framework. That the Library had to be preserved, but could no longer grow without order.

Rick Coleman accepted the outcome without celebration. Blue did not promise comfort, but it offered clarity. Julien Moreau and Sebastian Volker did not dispute the data. They questioned the political impact. Mateo Krüger remained silent, fully aware of what the decision implied.

The Oracle's verdict was not a technical act.

It was an act of honesty.

Among all possible options, the Blue System offered the best probability of governing the entire Empire, not merely sustaining it. It was not perfect. It was not easy. But it was the only one that reduced future complexity without denying present reality.

It won by tenths.

It won by rigor.

It won because it was evaluated without concessions.

When the process ended, no one rose with relief.

There was a different sensation.

The sense of having crossed a threshold.

The Empire could no longer claim ignorance. It could no longer hide behind incomplete evaluations or partial decisions. The Oracle had seen everything that could be seen.

Now, obeying it or ignoring it would be a conscious choice.

And that choice would no longer be merely technical.

Chapter 21 — The Silent Rebellion

After the fall of the Emperor, Olympus did not celebrate.

Nor did it descend into open crisis.

What followed was something more complex, and therefore more dangerous: a strategic pause. Meetings continued, reports kept circulating, minor decisions were taken as usual. But on the central issue, transformation, no one spoke.

The silence was not empty.

It was deliberate.

Tomás Iriarte ascended to the throne with a discourse of stability. He did not challenge the Oracle. He did not invalidate the evaluation. He did not promise rupture. He spoke of continuity, of listening to all Provinces, of protecting the balance that had allowed the Empire to grow. His message was received with relief by those who feared immediate execution, and with caution by those who understood that indecision is also a form of governance.

The new Emperor did not deny the future.

He postponed it, elegantly.

One of his first decisions was to reorganize the inner circle. He did not remove existing figures. He added a new one.

He appointed a Chief of Staff, a role designed to centralize coordination, filter priorities, and act as a bridge between the throne and execution. The appointment was presented as a modernization of imperial governance.

The chosen figure was brilliant.

Well trained.

Eloquent.

But he had not grown within the Empire.

For many in Olympus, the decision passed almost unnoticed. The role carried no formal power over the Provinces. It did not govern systems or budgets directly. Its authority came from something more subtle: proximity to the Emperor.

And proximity, in times of transformation, is decisive.

When it was announced that this new figure would assume coordination of the digital transformation, the silence grew heavier.

There were no public objections.

There was no applause.

Héctor Salgado was among the few who immediately understood the risk. Not out of personal distrust, but out of historical experience. He knew that a transformation of that magnitude is not executed with intelligence alone, nor with enthusiasm.

It is executed with memory.

With scars.

With authority earned on the ground.

And that cannot be delegated easily.

Leonardo Figueroa also sensed the tension. The Oracle had spoken clearly. The decision had been made. But now execution was in the hands of someone who had not been part of the journey, who had not walked the plants, who had not listened to the operators of Red or Yellow.

He did not doubt his capability.

He doubted his operational legitimacy.

In the Provinces of the West, Rick Coleman received the news with practical skepticism.

"Who do we call when something fails?" he asked.

"The throne, or the cabinet?"

It was not a rhetorical question.

It was a warning.

In the Provinces of the East, the reaction was different.

The new figure was seen as an opportunity. A fresh interlocutor, without prior history, without commitments to past decisions. Someone with whom a different narrative could be built around pace, scope, and priority of the transformation.

The silence of Olympus was beginning to find unintended allies.

Tomás Iriarte observed everything with calculated attention. He knew that executing the Oracle's verdict without breaking the balance required intermediaries. Figures capable of absorbing friction. Voices that could translate transformation into political language.

From his perspective, the appointment was logical.

From the Empire's history, it was risky.

Olympus did not block the transformation.

Nor did it drive it forward.

It left it suspended in an ambiguous space, where everyone knew it had to happen, but no one was willing to carry the full political cost. The new cabinet offered a temporary solution: advance without accelerating, transform without breaking.

The problem was that systems do not change in silence.

Héctor understood something unsettling.

The technical decision had survived the change of Emperor.

But its execution had become trapped in a new political layer, even more complex than the last.

The risk was no longer choosing poorly.

It was executing correctly under fragile leadership.

And in that carefully managed silence, the Empire moved dangerously close to a truth no one wanted to speak aloud:

A correct transformation, poorly led, can be more dangerous than no transformation at all.

Chapter 22 — The Power Vacuum

The decision was not announced as a victory.

When the Oracle's verdict became clear, there were no triumphant statements, nor discreet celebrations. There was no open resistance either. What followed was something far more dangerous: silence.

A silence heavy with calculation.

Emperor Adrián Valcázar understood immediately that the problem was no longer technical. The Empire had done what few organizations dared to do: look at itself without filters and choose the most coherent path, even if it was not the most comfortable one.

But that coherence carried a political cost.

In Olympus, the decision was received with courtesy. No one questioned the methodology. No one attacked the Oracle. No one discredited the work of Héctor Salgado or Leonardo Figueroa. The process had been so exhaustive that doing so would have lacked credibility.

The criticism took another form.

Questions.

Not about what, but about when.

Not about why, but about impact.

Not about the decision, but about execution.

The debate shifted with surgical elegance.

Mateo Krüger was among the first to set the tone.

"The decision is solid," he said. "But the Empire needs stability. Executing it now could generate unnecessary tension."

He was not speaking about systems.

He was speaking about power.

Sebastian Volker reinforced the message from another angle. He pointed out that the Eastern Provinces were not culturally prepared for a transformation of that magnitude. That forcing the pace could erode trust built over many years.

"A change like this requires consensus," he stated. "And consensus takes time."

No one contradicted him.

In the Western Provinces, Rick Coleman reacted with contained pragmatism. He accepted the outcome and even acknowledged its logic. But the timeline concerned him. The Empire could not afford operational failures while leadership was changing direction.

"If we are going to do this," he said, "let's do it properly. Without rushing."

It was a reasonable position.

And for that very reason, a dangerous one.

Adrián listened to all those voices carefully. He did not defend himself. He did not counterattack. He knew that Olympus was no longer debating the decision. It was debating whether he was the right person to execute it.

The Emperor represented something uncomfortable.

He was the one who had allowed the Oracle to speak.

And the one willing to obey it.

That made him a risk.

Héctor Salgado perceived the shift before many others. As Librarian, he was accustomed to reading weak signals. He saw conversations drifting, agendas being rearranged, certain meetings no longer including the Emperor without formal explanation.

There was no explicit conspiracy.

There was gradual alignment.

Leonardo Figueroa noticed it as well. The Oracle continued to be cited, but increasingly as a technical reference rather than a strategic mandate. The verdict was beginning to be treated as just another recommendation, not as a point of no return.

The risk was not that the decision would be rejected.

It was that it would be diluted.

Adrián understood then that his position had become untenable.

Not because he had failed.

But because he had been too clear.

In an Empire accustomed to living with ambiguity, someone willing to execute a shared truth disrupts the balance. He does not provoke immediate rejection. He provokes defensive caution.

And when caution organizes itself, it becomes replacement.

Olympus did not need to vote. It was enough to redefine priorities, accelerate conversations about "new phases" and "leadership aligned with the future." The language was impeccable. No one spoke of removal. They spoke of an orderly transition.

The assassination was political.

And precisely for that reason, perfect.

Adrián Valcázar left the throne without resistance. He knew that clinging to power would only have weakened the decision he had set in motion. His departure preserved something more important than his position: the legitimacy of the Oracle.

When the news was confirmed, the Empire reacted with a mixture of relief and disorientation.

Relief, because conflict had not erupted.

Disorientation, because the most important decision still awaited execution.

The new Emperor, Tomás Iriarte, assumed leadership in that ambiguous context. He inherited an Empire with a decision already made, and an Olympus not yet ready to live with its consequences.

The fall of the Emperor did not cancel the prophecy.

It postponed it.

But postponement is not neutral. It is a form of decision.

And as the Empire reorganized around its new leader, a question hovered without a clear answer:

Had the Emperor fallen for daring to change the system…

or for having revealed a truth the Empire was not prepared to accept?

Chapter 23 — The New Emperor

Tomás Iriarte did not ascend the throne wrapped in epic imagery.

There were no promises of refoundation, no speeches of rupture. His rise was orderly, almost technical, as if the Empire wanted to convince itself that nothing essential had changed. The transition was presented as institutional continuity, not as a course correction.

And, in a sense, it was.

The new Emperor inherited a peculiar Empire.

He did not arrive to decide the future. That work had already been done. The Oracle had spoken, the evaluation had been complete, and the technical decision was already taken. Tomás arrived to govern after the truth, not before it.

That detail defined everything.

In his first address to Olympus, Tomás chose every word carefully.

He spoke of listening.

Of integrating perspectives.

Of advancing responsibly.

He did not mention systems.

He did not mention timelines.

He did not mention the Blue path.

His speech reassured many.

For those who feared immediate execution, Tomás represented prudence. For those who had supported the fallen Emperor, he represented uncertainty. The new leader did not reject the transformation, but neither did he embrace it with urgency.

He kept it suspended.

One of his first actions was to reaffirm the role of the Chief of Staff.

Not as an executor, but as a strategic coordinator. The message was clear: the transformation would follow an orderly, mediated, carefully managed path. Nothing would be imposed without sufficient consensus.

The Empire exhaled.

But it did not move.

Héctor Salgado observed the move with quiet unease.

As Librarian, he understood the value of stability. But he also knew that the Empire's history was full of correct decisions neutralized by timid execution. Technical clarity, without firm political backing, tended to dissolve.

Tomás did not deny the decision.

He reinterpreted it.

Leonardo Figueroa was more pragmatic.

The Oracle had fulfilled its function. It was not his role to demand obedience. But he was troubled by the language beginning to circulate in Olympus: "exploratory phase," "cultural alignment," "impact review."

Legitimate words.

Also dangerous ones.

In the Western Provinces, Rick Coleman assessed the new Emperor with caution.

He appreciated moderation. He knew that a poorly executed transformation could damage operations. But he also sensed that the absence of clear direction would prolong uncertainty.

"A system does not change on its own," he said. "And operations do not wait indefinitely."

In the Eastern Provinces, the atmosphere was different.

Tomás was seen as an opportunity. A new leader, without direct commitment to the prior decision, could open space to renegotiate pace, scope, and priorities. The language of consensus felt familiar and comfortable.

Transformation became negotiable again.

Tomás understood those readings.

He was not naïve. He knew that governing after such a charged decision required balance. Push too hard and risk fractures. Move too slowly and risk irrelevance.

He chose a third path: managing ambiguity.

The new Emperor did not cancel the prophecy.

He turned it into an agenda.

An agenda without clear dates. Without single owners. Without a definitive narrative. Every step had to be validated, discussed, and adjusted. The goal was not to deny change, but to make it digestible.

But prolonged digestion also exhausts.

Héctor perceived then a risk greater than open disagreement.

The risk that the decision would become abstract. That the Oracle would cease to be a mandate and become a reference document. That the truth, once known, would lose urgency.

The Empire knew what to do.

But it no longer knew when.

Tomás Iriarte was not a villain.

He was a prudent ruler in an imprudent moment. His strength, the ability to reconcile, could become his greatest weakness if the Empire confused consensus with paralysis.

The new Emperor did not destroy the transformation.

He placed it on ground where it would either survive...

or slowly fade.

This chapter does not judge Tomás.

It observes him.

Governing after an uncomfortable truth is harder than governing before it. The Empire was entering a different phase of its history. It was no longer about deciding, but about daring to execute.

And that decision, the hardest of all, had not yet been made.

Chapter 24 — The Heir Without Scars

The heir did not arrive with thunder.

There was no solemn proclamation, no public ritual. His presence was felt first in the corridors, in agendas that quietly changed hands, in meetings where it was no longer clear who was taking notes and who was making decisions.

The Empire did not know him well.

But the Emperor trusted him.

And in Empires, that is often enough.

The heir had an impeccable education.

He had studied in the finest circles, spoke fluently the language of modernity, and discussed transformation, efficiency, and the future with ease. His ideas were clear, his arguments persuasive, his energy undeniable.

He did not lack intelligence.

He lacked history.

He had not lived through the crises that had shaped the Empire. He had not been present when systems survived through improvisation. He had not negotiated with halted plants nor defended decisions before dissatisfied Provinces.

He had no scars.

For the Emperor, that was an advantage.

He saw in the heir a clean mind, untouched by inertia or past commitments. Someone capable of executing change without the emotional weight that paralyzed others.

"We need a fresh perspective," he said more than once.

And he was not wrong.

The problem was not freshness.

It was depth.

Héctor Salgado observed the heir with professional curiosity.

As Librarian, he had seen many promising figures pass through the Empire. He knew that knowledge is not always transmitted through degrees or speeches. Some forms of understanding are acquired only when something fails and one must respond.

The heir listened attentively, but he did not yet distinguish between warning and resistance. To him, many objections sounded like fear of change rather than institutional memory.

It was not arrogance.

It was inexperience.

Leonardo Figueroa tried to build bridges.

He explained the Oracle's process, the rigor with which the decision had been constructed, the reasons why the Blue System had been chosen by tenths rather than enthusiasm. The heir understood the arguments, but he did not yet feel their weight.

To him, transformation was a project.

To others, it was an open wound.

In the Western Provinces, Rick Coleman was direct.

"We are not worried about the future," he told him.

"We are worried about the line starting tomorrow."

He did not say it defiantly.

He said it realistically.

The heir nodded, took notes, promised coordination. But he did not yet understand that on the shop floor, every unfulfilled promise leaves a mark. That credibility is not built with plans, but with presence.

In the Eastern Provinces, the reading was different.

The heir represented an opportunity. Unbound by past decisions, he could be persuaded. Without scars, he could accept carefully crafted narratives about local particularities, different timelines, and strategic priorities.

It was not overt manipulation.

It was subtle influence.

The heir listened to all voices with equal attention, still unable to distinguish which spoke from experience and which from convenience.

Olympus watched in silence.

Some saw promise in the heir. Others saw risk. But no one was willing to openly confront a decision made by a newly crowned Emperor. The balance remained fragile.

Meanwhile, transformation advanced in documents, presentations, and committees...

but not in reality.

Héctor then understood the paradox.

The Empire had chosen the right path.

It had invested time, rigor, and honesty in deciding.

But it had now delegated execution to a figure who did not yet understand the invisible cost of change. Someone without scars does not fear repeating mistakes...

because they do not yet know how much they hurt.

The heir was not the villain.

He was the reflection of a dangerous belief: that transformation can be executed without passing through the past. That will and method alone are enough to change systems that have sustained an Empire for decades.

History shows otherwise.

Real transformations require more than vision.

They require respect for what has already bled.

The chapter closed without open conflict.

But with a clear tension.

The Empire was about to begin its greatest technological transformation...

led by someone who had not yet learned to recognize the warning signs that only scars can leave.

And that combination, a correct decision with fragile execution, was the most dangerous of all.

Chapter 25 — The Real Challenge

The Empire had made its decision.

That alone was exceptional.

It had examined its systems, its numbers, and its contradictions without disguise. It had listened to the Oracle. It had accepted that the Blue System offered the best possible balance between order, future, and governability.

But deciding is not transforming.

For weeks, Olympus repeated the same phrase with different nuances:

"The hardest part is over."

It was a dangerous illusion.

Héctor Salgado knew it.

As Librarian, he had witnessed many attempts at change over the years. He knew that important decisions rarely fail at the moment they are made. They fail later, when they must be executed in a world that continues to operate while it changes.

The real challenge was not technological.

It never had been.

The challenge was to build a shared truth without destroying daily operations. To design a common future without denying local histories. To govern without falling into the temptation to impose.

The Blue System was not coming to replace software.

It was coming to replace implicit agreements.

For decades, the Empire had operated under a logic of tolerated exceptions. Each Province had developed its own language to explain results, justify deviations, and prioritize investments. None of this was necessarily wrong, but none of it was comparable.

The Blue did not eliminate exceptions.

It made them visible.

And that changed everything.

Leonardo Figueroa explained it clearly in one of the first sessions after the decision:

"Implementation does not start when the system is installed. It starts when we agree on what 'normal' means."

The word unsettled the room.

Because defining normal meant deciding which practices would no longer be acceptable. Which shortcuts would no longer be justified. Which particularities would have to adapt to a common framework.

Rick Coleman understood the risk from an operational perspective.

"If we define that framework poorly," he warned, "the system will work, but the plant will not."

He was not speaking from resistance.

He was speaking from experience.

In the Eastern Provinces, the concern was different.

Julien Moreau saw in the global template a silent threat. Not because it was technically unfeasible, but because it reduced the space to negotiate local narratives. A common process implied common indicators. And common indicators eliminate gray areas.

Sebastian Volker expressed it diplomatically:

"A single model can ignore different realities."

He was right.

But it also avoided a key question: how many different realities can an Empire sustain before it ceases to be one?

The real challenge began to take shape when the discussion turned to the Template.

Not as a technical document.

As a cultural contract.

Defining a global template meant deciding how to purchase, how to produce, how to sell, and how to report across the entire Empire. It was not an imposition of the Blue System. It was a consequence of wanting to govern coherently.

Héctor insisted on something few wanted to hear:

"The template should not reflect the best plant. It should reflect the average plant, and allow improvement."

The silence was uncomfortable.

Because everyone knew that some Provinces would emerge better positioned than others. That some practices defended for years would not survive a common definition. That the template would not only organize processes, but also implicit hierarchies.

The challenge was not to design the perfect system.

It was to accept one that was sufficiently fair.

Before leaving the throne, Adrián Valcázar had left a clear warning:

"If we turn this into a war between Capital and Provinces, we lose."

Tomás Iriarte inherited that sentence as a burden.

He knew that the success of the transformation would not depend on the timeline or the vendor. It would depend on something far more fragile: trust. Trust that the change was not a punishment. Trust that the Blue was not meant to expose mistakes, but to make them correctable.

But trust cannot be decreed.

It is built through uncomfortable decisions, well justified exceptions, and clear boundaries. It is built when the Empire demonstrates that it is also willing to change from the Capital, not only from the Provinces.

The real challenge was not convincing those who opposed.

It was not disappointing those who had accepted.

Because a transformation that is announced and poorly executed does not merely fail. It leaves scars deeper than inertia ever could.

And as the Empire prepared to design its global template, a truth began to emerge with unsettling clarity:

Choosing the Blue System had been the easiest act of the entire process.

What was truly difficult was only just beginning.

Chapter 26 — The Template

The Template was not born as a document.

It was born as discomfort.

When the Blue System was selected, many within the Empire assumed that the next step would be technical: hiring implementers, defining timelines, scheduling deployments. But Héctor Salgado interrupted that momentum with a simple, almost unsettling question:

"What exactly are we going to implement?"

The room fell silent.

No one questioned the system.

What no one had yet defined was the common way of existing within it.

The Template was not a configuration.

It was a declaration of principles.

Defining it meant answering questions the Empire had avoided for years:

How do we truly procure?

When is a process standard, and when is it an exception?

What does it mean to "close a month"?

Which practices are part of identity, and which are merely habit?

Leonardo Figueroa explained it with clarity:

"The Template does not define how the best plant operates. It defines how any plant should be able to operate."

The discomfort was immediate.

Rick Coleman was the first to react.

"If we design this from a desk, we will fail," he said. "No plant is average when a line stops."

He was right.

But Héctor responded with an equally uncomfortable truth:

"And if we design it only from the plants, we will never have an Empire."

The Template had to walk a dangerous line:

common enough to govern, flexible enough to operate.

In the Eastern Provinces, the word "template" triggered a different kind of resistance. Julien Moreau understood exactly what it implied: a drastic reduction in interpretive margin. A single model meant explicit rules. And explicit rules leave little room for alternative narratives.

"A global template ignores context," he said. "Not everything can be standardized."

Sebastian Volker was more subtle.

"The risk is not the template," he argued. "The risk is using it as a tool of control rather than alignment."

Olympus listened.

Mateo Krüger added a historical perspective:

"Empires fall when they confuse uniformity with cohesion."

No one disputed that.

But Héctor insisted:

"And they also fall when they allow every territory to define its own truth."

The Template was not meant to standardize people.

It was meant to organize decisions.

For the first time, the Empire had to accept something uncomfortable: many differences long defended as "local necessities" were nothing more than isolated solutions to problems no one had been willing to resolve structurally.

The work of defining the Template forced difficult conversations.

Duplicated processes.

Missing controls.

Informal approvals that survived only because of age.

None of it was illegal.

But none of it was governable.

Héctor proposed a clear rule:

"The Template will not be negotiated in Olympus. It will be built with those who execute."

And so began an unprecedented exercise.

Teams from the Capital, the Western Provinces, and the Eastern Provinces sat at the same table, not to defend systems, but to explain realities. The Template ceased to be an abstract idea and became an uncomfortable mirror.

Some saw themselves reflected with pride.

Others, with surprise.

A few, with fear.

Because the Template did something no system had done before:

it turned implicit decisions into visible rules.

It did not punish.

But it did not allow hiding.

Leonardo observed how the debate evolved.

The discussion was no longer about which system to use.

It was about what kind of Empire they wanted to be.

An Empire where each Province operated as an efficient island.

Or one where all shared a common language, even at the cost of surrendering certain freedoms.

The Template did not resolve the conflict.

It made it explicit.

And that was its greatest contribution.

When the first draft was completed, no one celebrated.

It was not elegant.

It was not perfect.

But it was honest.

Héctor knew it the moment he saw it.

That document would not be liked.

It would hurt.

And precisely because of that, it would work.

Because the Template did not promise comfort.

It promised coherence.

And in an Empire accustomed to living with partial truths, coherence was the most radical change of all.

Chapter 27 — Changing Without Breaking

Héctor Salgado was not afraid of change.

He was afraid of how change is usually executed.

Before becoming the Empire's Librarian, he had witnessed and led other global transformations. Not all within this Empire. Some in organizations that believed changing systems was a technical problem rather than a human one. Projects that began with enthusiasm and ended in exhaustion, internal friction, and an invisible cost no one wanted to acknowledge.

In one of those implementations, the cost never appeared in the budget.

It appeared in his body.

Weeks without sleep. Urgent decisions made at the edge of exhaustion. Endless meetings where no one wanted to assume responsibility, yet everyone demanded results. Héctor had learned, in the hardest possible way, that poorly understood change management does not only break processes.

It breaks people.

That is why, when the Blue System was selected, his first reaction was not relief.

It was concern.

Changing without breaking was not a slogan.

It was a condition for survival.

"If we push too hard," he warned in Olympus, "the operation will defend itself. And when the operation defends itself, the system loses."

He was not speaking in abstractions.

He was speaking from memory.

The Empire had hundreds of processes that worked not because they were optimal, but because people had learned how to live with them. Every poorly communicated adjustment, every decision made without listening to the shop floor, could trigger silent resistance that no project plan ever detects.

Leonardo Figueroa agreed.

"The worst implementation," he said, "is the one that meets the timeline and fails in adoption."

The real challenge was not speed.

It was awareness.

Changing without breaking meant accepting something uncomfortable: not everything could be transformed at the same time. Not all Provinces were equally prepared. Not all leaders understood the impact of the Blue System with the same depth.

Rick Coleman said it plainly.

"If change puts production at risk, production will win."

It was not a threat.

It was an operational law.

In the Eastern Provinces, fragility took a different form. There, the risk was not stopping lines, but eroding local political agreements. Changing processes meant redefining roles, eliminating intermediaries, and exposing decisions that had previously been resolved without formal records.

Julien Moreau understood this perfectly.

"If we break too many things at once," he said, "no one will want to rebuild."

He was right.

Héctor then proposed a principle that made many uncomfortable.

"Change should not demonstrate power. It should demonstrate care."

Care for the operation.

Care for people.

Care for institutional memory.

The Blue System had to introduce order without humiliating the past. It could not present itself as the correction of historical mistakes, but as a necessary evolution. Every migrated process needed a clear reason. Every eliminated exception required an explanation that people could understand.

Changing without breaking demanded something few transformations are willing to accept:

the surrender of absolute control.

The Empire would have to allow gradual transitions, temporary coexistence, even controlled inconsistencies. Not as failures, but as adaptation mechanisms. The Blue System could not be imposed as dogma. It had to earn its place in daily reality.

Héctor insisted on protecting key teams.

"We cannot burn those who sustain the change," he said. "If we lose the guardians of knowledge, the system loses its soul."

No one responded immediately.

But everyone understood.

The change could not repeat the history of heroic projects that succeed on paper and devastate those who execute them. The Empire could not afford another transformation that was technically successful and humanly destructive.

Changing without breaking meant accepting imperfect rhythms, uneven progress, and decisions that prioritized stability over speed. It meant listening more than commanding. Adjusting more than imposing.

And above all, it meant recognizing an uncomfortable truth:

An Empire that survives change is not the one that transforms the fastest, but the one that manages to transform without losing those who make it possible.

Héctor knew this better than anyone.

His health, his history, and his scars were proof enough.

Chapter 28 — Resistance

Resistance did not arrive as a "no."

It arrived as full calendars.

As postponed meetings.

As decisions that needed "a little more analysis."

In the Empire, no one openly opposed the Blue System. That would have been too visible. Resistance was more intelligent than that. More sophisticated. It hid behind reasonable words: prudence, operational care, cultural respect.

The transformation had been approved.

But the energy to execute it began to dissipate.

Héctor Salgado noticed it before most.

Not in reports.

In silences.

Teams that once responded quickly now asked for additional clarification. Local leaders requested temporary exceptions that never seemed to expire. Template definitions were accepted... with footnotes.

Nothing serious.

Nothing confrontational.

But constant.

Leonardo Figueroa called it by its real name.

"This isn't disagreement," he said. "It's passive friction."

Rick Coleman experienced it from operations.

"No one is against it," he said. "But every week there's a new reason not to move forward."

In the Western Provinces, resistance took a pragmatic form. Operational risks were cited. Demand peaks. Competing priorities. Each argument was valid on its own. The problem was the pattern: there was always something more urgent than the transformation.

It was not bad faith.

It was survival.

In the Eastern Provinces, resistance was more structured.

Julien Moreau understood that the Blue System could not be blocked directly. So he surrounded it with caution. He proposed limited pilots, extended evaluations, additional comparative analyses. None of this stopped the project.

But it slowed it enough to buy time.

Sebastian Volker added a higher narrative.

"Transformation must mature organically."

It was an elegant phrase.

And a dangerously empty one.

Mateo Krüger observed from Olympus with a mix of understanding and calculation. He knew that all transformations generate resistance. But he also knew that without clear pressure from the top, resistance eventually sets its own pace.

The problem was not resistance.

It was the absence of counterweight.

The heir without scars tried to intervene.

He called meetings. Asked for commitment. Spoke of shared vision. His tone was correct. His speech inspiring. But it lacked something essential: authority forged through conflict.

When someone has not lived the consequences of a bad decision, urgency sounds theoretical.

Héctor tried to warn him.

"Resistance cannot be eliminated," he said. "It is managed through presence."

Emails and committees were not enough. The Empire needed visible decisions. Clear priorities. Explicit renunciations. Every exception granted without limits reinforced the idea that change was optional.

The Template began to fragment.

Not by design.

By concession.

Some Provinces asked to adapt processes "temporarily." Others requested to keep satellite systems "until further notice." Each request was reasonable. Together, they formed a map of silent resistance.

Leonardo summarized it bluntly.

"We are designing the system of the future while operating under the rules of the past."

The risk was not failure.

It was dilution.

Resistance did not seek to defeat change.

It sought to exhaust it.

And it knew how to wait.

Héctor had seen that ending before.

Transformations that do not collapse, but never consolidate. Projects that survive long enough to be labeled "in progress" for years, until context shifts and urgency fades.

And then, everything begins again.

The Empire was still in time.

But the clock was no longer measuring months or phases.

It was measuring credibility.

Every week without visible progress weakened the Oracle's mandate. Every postponed decision turned transformation into yet another promise. And promises repeated without execution eventually become noise.

Resistance did not shout.

It whispered.

And in that constant whisper, the Empire began to face its most uncomfortable truth:

It is not enough to decide correctly.

One must sustain the decision when it stops being popular.

Chapter 29 — The Invisible Guardians

The cost of change is not paid only in budgets.

For years, someone had already been paying it in silence.

They were never mentioned in the early discussions. They did not appear in strategic presentations or Olympus speeches. They did not lead committees or sign final decisions. Yet when something failed, and something always failed, they were the first to be called.

They were the Guardians.

They did not protect thrones or visible treasures. They protected something far more fragile: the Empire's daily operation. They knew every improvised integration, every tolerated exception, every patch applied at midnight so production could start at dawn. They knew which processes were documented... and which existed only because someone remembered them.

The Guardians did not make strategic decisions.

They survived them.

For years, they had sustained the Empire quietly. When a Province grew faster than expected, they found a way to scale without breaking. When an acquisition brought incompatible systems, they stitched together temporary solutions that became permanent. When a report did not reconcile, they understood why before anyone asked.

Their knowledge was not in manuals.

It was in scars.

In Olympus, stability was discussed as if it were a natural quality of the Empire. Few understood that this stability had names and faces, even if they were rarely spoken. The Guardians were summoned for battles, not for celebrations. They were asked for endurance, not recognition. For fast answers, not opinions.

They were useful in crisis.

Invisible in calm.

When Project Matrix began to take shape, many assumed the Guardians would be natural allies. After all, no one knew the cracks of the Red system or the real limits of the Yellow better than they did. But that assumption ignored something essential: accumulated exhaustion.

Héctor Salgado understood this well.

Not only as the Librarian, but as someone who had lived through other global transformations. He knew what it meant to carry an implementation that promised order while generating temporary chaos. He knew how sustained stress, urgent decisions, and responsibility without authority erode even the most committed teams.

He had seen colleagues fall ill.

He had seen marriages strain.

He had seen talent leave quietly, not for lack of ability, but for lack of meaning.

The Guardians did not fear change.

They feared repeating a familiar story: being called to extinguish fires others had ignited, being held responsible without being heard, being experts without a voice.

For many of them, the Blue System represented a painful paradox. On one hand, it promised coherence, traceability, and an architecture that would finally make visible what they had been holding together by force of will for years. On the other, it implied a deep transformation that would once again rest on their shoulders.

"Us again," some thought.

Again, weekends. Long nights. Urgent decisions with no margin for error.

In the Provinces, the perception was even harsher. Local Guardians knew that when something went wrong, it would not be Olympus that responded. It would be them. In front of operators, supervisors, and managers who did not distinguish between a strategic decision and a technical failure, the visible face of change was always the same.

And yet, they were rarely invited to decide.

The Empire spoke of cultural transformation, but continued to treat operational knowledge as a utilitarian resource. Something to be consumed, not protected. Something that responds, not questions.

Some Guardians began to leave.

Not with scandal.

Not with reproach.

They simply stopped being available.

It was not a mass exodus, but it was significant. Each departure carried years of undocumented memory, tacit decisions, fine-grained understanding that no system could immediately capture. The Empire noticed late, when certain problems began to take longer to resolve, when answers stopped being immediate.

The cost did not appear in budgets.

It appeared in silence.

Héctor insisted on something few wanted to hear: transformation could not be sustained without the Guardians. Not as executors, but as real participants in the conversation. Asking for commitment was not enough. Something had to be offered in return: recognition, voice, protection from burnout.

"We cannot ask them to cross the bridge," he said, "if we are not willing to walk with them."

But the Empire does not always listen to those who speak from the trenches. Sometimes it confuses resilience with infinite availability. It confuses vocation with obligation.

The Invisible Guardians did not seek protagonism.

They sought respect.

Because they knew something many preferred to ignore: no system, no matter how coherent, survives a poorly accompanied transformation. No architecture holds if those who sustain it feel expendable. No Empire transforms itself by ignoring those who keep it standing when no one is watching.

Project Matrix would move forward.

With or without them.

But the true risk was not technical.

It was human.

And in that silent risk, the Empire faced an uncomfortable truth:

The Invisible Guardians do not fail when they leave.

The Empire fails when it stops seeing them.

When the Empire finally chose to look into a shared mirror, it did not discover something new.

It discovered, at last, what the Invisible Guardians had known all along.

Chapter 30 — The First Mirror

The first mirror was not a report.

It did not arrive as an official document or a carefully polished presentation for Olympus. It arrived in a far simpler way, and for that reason, far more unsettling: a consolidated view.

A single screen.

A single language.

A single set of numbers.

Nothing new.

Nothing unknown.

But never before seen this way.

When the first consolidation exercise under the Template was ready, no one asked to celebrate it. There were no mass emails or solemn announcements. Héctor Salgado shared it cautiously, like someone revealing an X-ray that confirms a long-avoided suspicion.

"This is only a reflection," he said. "Not a conclusion."

But everyone understood it was more than that.

The mirror did not accuse.

It did not explain.

It did not justify.

It showed.

For the first time, the Empire could observe its operations as a coherent whole. The Western and Eastern Provinces appeared under the same rules, the same indicators, the same criteria of comparison.

The numbers were not wrong. But they were no longer comfortably separated.

Rick Coleman was among the first to review the data.

He did not look for errors.

He looked for context.

"There's history missing here," he said.

And he was right.

An isolated figure does not explain a decision made during a crisis at dawn, sustained by people who never appear on the screen. It does not reflect a production line stopped by a failed supplier, nor an exception approved to protect a strategic customer. The mirror showed results, not trajectories.

And yet, the impact was immediate.

Some Provinces recognized themselves with pride. Others with surprise. A few with quiet unease. Not because the numbers were incorrect, but because they no longer allowed flexible interpretation.

Julien Moreau observed the mirror with controlled attention.

What he saw was not an error.

It was the loss of narrative control.

For years, results could be explained through local singularity. Now that singularity still existed, but it could no longer hide behind different structures. The mirror did not contradict stories. It aligned them.

Sebastian Volker was more reflective.

"This is going to change conversations," he said.

He was not talking about technology.

He was talking about power.

Mateo Krüger understood the scope immediately.

An Empire that sees itself without filters cannot pretend ignorance. Every future decision would be accompanied by an unavoidable reference: what was already known.

The mirror did not force action.

But it made not knowing impossible.

The heir without scars watched the screen with a mixture of fascination and caution. For the first time, he understood that transformation was not a project, but a progressive exposure. Each advance of the Blue System would expand the mirror. Each integrated process would reduce the ability to explain results without shared data.

Héctor noticed.

"This is only the beginning," he told him. "The second mirror hurts more."

He did not say it as a threat.

He said it as a warning.

The first mirror did not resolve conflicts.

It revealed them.

It did not impose decisions.

It made them inevitable.

And above all, it changed something fundamental in the Empire: the conversation stopped revolving around perceptions and began revolving around comparable facts. Not definitive, but shared.

The silence that followed was not resistance.

134

It was assimilation.

Everyone understood that the mirror could not be broken without breaking the Empire's coherence itself. It could be ignored, yes. But it would become increasingly obvious when it was.

The transformation had crossed an invisible threshold.

It was no longer an intention.

It was a presence.

And as Olympus and the Provinces withdrew to process what they had seen, one truth lingered without needing to be spoken:

The Blue System had not changed the Empire.

The Empire had begun to see itself as it truly was.

And once an Empire sees itself without filters,

returning to darkness ceases to be an option.

Epilogue — It was never an ERP

It never was.

Even though that is how it began.

Even though that is how it was presented.

Even though that is how it was defended in meetings, budgets, and timelines.

For a long time, the Empire believed it was choosing a system. A set of modules, integrated processes, standardized reports. It believed the debate was technological, that the conflict would be resolved through architecture, vendors, and go-live dates.

But the system was only the pretext.

What was truly at stake was something far deeper:

Who had the right to define the truth.

For years, the Empire had functioned thanks to a delicate balance between local realities and global narratives. Each Province operated, produced, and sold according to its own rules, while the Capital consolidated plausible stories. Not false. But incomplete. Just enough for everyone to coexist without confronting what they preferred not to see.

That was not corruption.

It was organizational survival.

The Blue System did not arrive to correct errors. It arrived to eliminate ambiguities. And ambiguities, uncomfortable as they may be to admit, are often the silent lubricant of power.

The Oracle did not choose a system.

It chose coherence.

And coherence, in a large Empire, always has consequences.

In the end, no one lost their throne overnight. No one was publicly exposed. There were no clear villains and no obvious winners. What emerged instead was something far harder to manage: gradual exposure.

The Empire began to see itself.

And seeing itself changed the conversations.

Some resistances softened. Others adapted. Some learned to live with the mirror. Others searched for new shadows. The change was neither linear nor clean. It never is.

But something could no longer be undone.

Once the Empire understood that it could operate with a single version of the truth, accepting multiple truths ceased to be an innocent option. Every exception began to demand justification. Every local narrative required context. Every decision required traceability.

Power changed its shape.

It did not concentrate.

It became visible.

And that, for any organization, is a transformation far deeper than any technological migration.

Perhaps one day the Blue System will be replaced.

Perhaps another generation will debate new platforms, new models, new colors. That is inevitable. Systems pass. Architectures evolve.

But the decision that defined this Empire was not technological.

It was ethical.

To choose to see itself without filters.

To accept uncomfortable comparisons.

To govern with shared data, even when it hurt.

That was the real change.

That is why this book is not about ERP.

It is about power.

About fear.

About memory.

And about the fragile courage required to sustain a shared truth.

Because in the end, systems do not transform Empires.

Empires transform when they decide to stop lying to themselves.

About the Author

José Antonio González Villalón is a technology executive and transformation leader with experience in high-impact strategic decision-making within complex, global organizations.

He has led and advised large-scale transformation initiatives across multiple industries.

His work focuses on leadership, technology governance, and organizational transformation, exploring the human, cultural, and ethical factors that determine the success or failure of critical decisions.

Matrix: The Impossible Decision is his first corporate novel.

Author's Note for Executives

This book was written for those who have had to decide when no comfortable option existed.

For those who have chaired committees where every argument was reasonable, but not all could be honored. For those who have felt the weight of a decision that was correct, yet still met with resistance. For those who understand that leadership is not about choosing between good and evil, but between incomplete truths.

If you currently hold — or have held — a leadership position, you will likely recognize more than one situation described in these pages. Not because events unfolded exactly this way, but because the patterns repeat themselves. Names change. Geographies change. Technologies change. The tensions, however, remain remarkably consistent.

This is not a book against prudence.

It is a book against paralysis disguised as prudence.

Nor is it a book against local autonomy or operational diversity. It is a book about the limits of that autonomy when it begins to compete with coherence, transparency, and institutional sustainability.

Many transformations fail not due to a lack of analysis, but because of excessive negotiation after the decision has already been made. Evaluation is rigorous, the decision is taken with courage... and execution follows with fear. In that space between decision and action, projects dissolve, teams burn out, and credibility erodes.

This book does not aim to tell you which decision to make.

That depends on your context, your industry, and your moment in time.

What it does aim to do is invite reflection on three questions that are rarely asked with full honesty:

What truths does your organization avoid because they are uncomfortable?

How much of your current complexity is legitimate legacy, and how much is accumulated postponement?

Are you willing to stand by a decision once it stops being popular?

Technology, in this story, is merely the catalyst. The real subject is the exercise of power when information can no longer be negotiated. When data begins to speak a common language, and narratives must adapt to it.

If, upon finishing this book, you feel validated in some past decisions, that is fine.

If you feel uneasy about certain reflections, even better.

Discomfort is often the first symptom of conscious leadership.

This book does not offer solutions.

It offers mirrors.

And what each organization chooses to do after looking into them... no longer depends on the author.